THE BLACK GOLD MOB

ALSO BY MARK GREATHOUSE

The Frontier Chronicles

Perilous Trails

Wyoming Calls

Longhorns North

Warpath

Hunter Vs. Hunted

Freedom Drovers

A Poison Spreads

Darkness Looms

The Tumbleweed Sagas

Nueces Justice

Nueces Reprise

Nueces Deceit

Nueces Blood

Nueces Grit

Nueces Truth

Nueces Legend

The Tumbleweed Sagas: Junior's Story

Lone Star Vigilante: Justice Texas Style

Guns on the Guadalupe: Justice on the River

Railroad to Perdition: Justice Rides an Iron Horse

THE BLACK GOLD MOB

CAPPING A CRIME GUSHER

THE TUMBLEWEED SAGAS
BOOK 11

MARK GREATHOUSE

The Black Gold Mob: Capping a Crime Gusher
Paperback Edition

Wolfpack Publishing
1707 E. Diana Street
Tampa, Florida 33610

www.wolfpackpublishing.com

Paperback ISBN 979-8-89567-522-9
Ebook ISBN 979-8-89567-521-2

Dedicated with love to my wife, Carolyn, and to our two sons, Mike and Matt.

THE NUECES STRIP

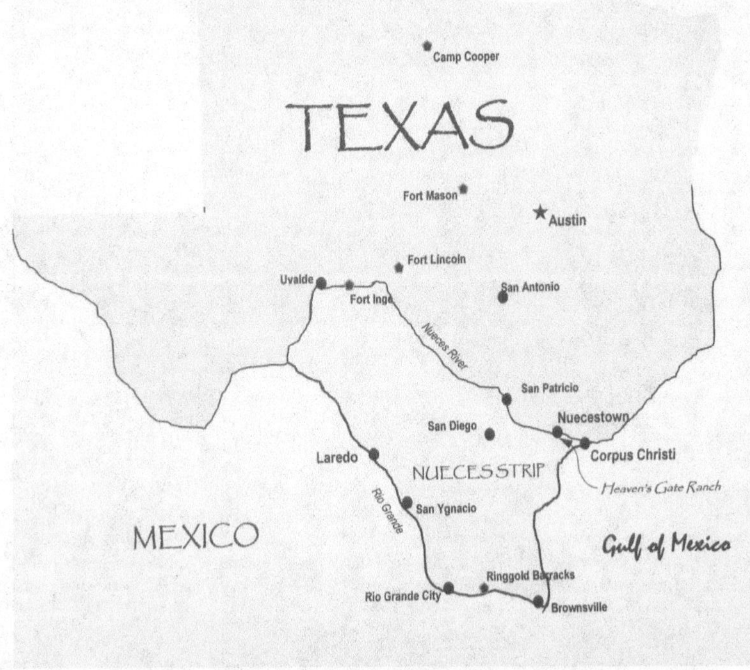

The vast Nueces Strip serves as the primary setting for the Tumbleweed Sagas. The Strip was also called Wild Horse Desert, owing to the millions of Mustangs that roamed its prairies. *(Sketch by Mark Greathouse)*

NUECESTOWN

Nuecestown, Texas, established in 1852 by English and German settlers, was developed by Corpus Christi founder Colonel Henry Kinney along the Nueces River as a ferry crossing. Mostly thanks to the railroad passing it by, it's now a "ghost town" marked only by historical markers. All that remains is a preserved schoolhouse and the old Nuecestown Cemetery. By 1896, the town was struggling economically due to the railroads passing it by. *(Sketch by Mark Greathouse)*

THE CAST

Lucas Dunn Jr.—*Goes by the nickname* **Junior**. *The proverbial fruit doesn't grow far from the tree, as Junior follows in the lawman footsteps of his legendary Texas Ranger father.*

Cassie McCully Dunn—*Daughter of Grant McCully, who owns a ranch near Heaven's Gate. Cassie is married to Junior. Children are Sean and Bode.*

Lucas "Long Luke" Dunn—*Was one of the greatest Texas Ranger Captains ever, having gained repute as an Indian fighter and respected lawman. Comanche called him Ghost-Who-Rides. Luke builds Heaven's Gate Ranch and has eleven children with his wife Elisa.*

Elisa Corrigan Dunn—*Married Luke Dunn after losing her family to frontier rigors, including fighting off Comanche and hired killers.*

Brody & Tess—*Junior's blue lacy dogs.*

Kyle McClintock—*Hired gun and jealous friend of Junior Dunn.*

Gordon Murphy—*Financier from New York City with interests in oil and railroads. Connected with the Irish Mob.*

Colin O'Neal—*Second in command to Gordon Murphy and Irish Mob enforcer.*

Karl Aimes—*Financial advisor to Corsicana Mayor James Woods.*

Lilly—*Bargirl at the Iron Front Saloon in Corsicana, TX.*

Ernest Carson—*President of the Dallas Trust, a bank serving the Irish Mob.*

Matilda Haskell—*Wife of a cattle, cotton, and hopeful oil baron of north Texas.*

George—*Muscle hired by Gordon Murphy for security.*

Pedro Martinez—*Ranch hand at Heaven's Gate Ranch.*

Jimmy Donovan—*Ranch hand at Heaven's Gate Ranch.*

Jake Carswell—*Former King Ranch cowboy hired as a ranch hand at Heaven's Gate Ranch.*

Carlos Arturo Mayor—*Mexican revolutionary.*

Chato—*Rogue Apache bent on avenging his oppressed people.*

HISTORICAL CHARACTERS

Charles Culberson—*Followed Jim Hogg and then Joseph Clay Stiles Blackburn as governor of Texas. He ran afoul of the Democratic Party over his opposition to the Ku Klux Klan.*

John Reynolds Hughes—*Became the longest-serving Texas Ranger captain.*

Hughes dealt with Comanche and Apache over his years as a rancher and lawman. He was a sergeant in the Frontier Battalion down along the Texas/Mexico border until 1893, when he was promoted to captain.

Archer Parr—*Known as "Archie," he established a political dynasty in what became Jim Wells County and led to decades of Democratic Party control through means fair and foul.*

Stephen Powers—*Political power broker exercising tight control over goings on in Corpus Christi. He has close ties with Archie Parr and Jim Wells.*

John McTiernan—*Sheriff of Nueces County, TX from 1896 to 1902.*

Uriah Lott—*Railroad entrepreneur who founded several railroads in Texas.*

John H. Reagan—*First chairman of the Railroad Commission of Texas.*

John Hillard Dunn—*Railroad entrepreneur and lifelong railroad man.*

John "Red John" Dunn—*Retired Texas Ranger who rode with Captains Wallace and McNelly.*

Robert Kleberg—*Married Alice Gertrudis King and became the owner of the huge King Ranch.*

William H. Miller—*US Marshall for the Northern District of Texas in 1898*

William H. Moon—*Dallas County sheriff from 1898 to 1900.*

James Hollins Woods—*Mayor of Corsicana, Texas, in 1898.*

Robert Allen—*Navarro County sheriff in 1898, based in Corsicana, Texas.*

THEME

JUSTICE

The quality of being just, impartial, or fair per the principle or ideal of just dealing or proper action in conformance to a principle or ideal as defined by the law or to truth, fact, or reason.

YOU'RE INVITED

Howdy,

With Tumbleweed Sagas: Junior's Story, I'm right pleased to have taken up where the story of my legendary dad left off, as he brought lawbreakers to justice as a Texas Ranger. I expect it runs strong in my ancestral blood.

The Black Gold Mob: Capping a Crime Gusher picks up my story from *Railroad to Perdition: Justice Rides an Iron Horse.* Like the prequels, it offers a twisted tale of intrigue in my attempt to solve a series of murders and land grabs. The Irish Mafia is mixed up in it somehow. The Nueces Strip, encompassing the southern tip of Texas by this time, could be said to be afire economically, as agriculture, railroads, communications, and black gold spawned ever greater growth.

Communications? While the telegraph expanded its reach, it was the soon-to-be-ubiquitous telephone that was beginning to make its presence felt mostly in the larger Texas cities. And black gold? That's Texas crude. The "Lucas Gusher" at Spindletop Hill, a couple of years off in 1901 near Beaumont, would eventually usher in the Texas oil era. Gushers of oil would become ever more common, sending geysers of money into bank accounts. Meanwhile, forces were jockeying to take advantage of the anticipated oil boom.

It's 1898, and the Nueces Strip could be inhospitable six ways to Sunday. Mottes or small clusters of live oak or mesquite offered occasional shade relief on the sunbaked prairies. The often-dry creek beds and arroyos eventually filled with rainwater and emptied into Nueces Bay and... farther to the east...Corpus Christi Bay. Flash flooding was an ongoing fear. Summers? Well, they tended to be hot and humid. Weather was pretty much whatever you wanted, if you waited long enough.

The abundant animal life on the Nueces Strip featured deer, javelina, fox, coyote, lynx, black bear, and mountain lion. Armadillos and prairie dogs competed for prairie real estate. At one point, horses were more numerous on the Strip than any animal, including humans. Occasionally, spotted ocelots and even wolves could be sighted by the practiced eye. Owls, hawks, eagles, buzzards...they abounded. Come spring, wildflowers swept across much of the landscape, painted like a huge rainbow, with scarlet sage, hibiscus, daisies, poppies, lilies, and the ubiquitous bluebonnets. Groves of cypress, juniper, and palmetto could be found. Pecan trees drew their sustenance from rich soil along the Nueces River. The very name *nueces* was Spanish for nuts. Cactus, along with yucca and agave, abounded. The Nueces Strip surely served as God's canvas.

If you were on foot, it was advisable to keep an eye and ear peeled for rattlesnakes. They tended to blend in fairly well with their surroundings, so their rattle was often folks' first and only warning of an impending attack. The rattlesnake spawned many a "Texas-ism" like "he's so bad he has rattlesnake fangs and twice the venom" or "he's so tough, he cuddles with rattlesnakes."

The similarities between natural and human dangers were often striking. Imagine the intense yellow eyes and tense muscles of a mountain lion on the hunt. A doe looks about innocently unaware. The lion's tail twitches ever-so-slightly. Patience...of sorts. The moment of attack must be exactly right. Only that infinitesimal twitch of the tip of his tail reveals the tension as he is about to launch himself. He dares not indulge even a blink of eyes. The doe sniffs the air and dips her head to feed. The mountain lion's muscled haunches spring him forward with claws splayed. His jaws grasp the doe's neck in a death grip. In its vast silence, the Nueces Strip sucks it all in. Danger was a constant.

Application of the law could too often be horrifically fast or mind-bogglingly slow. The accused lawbreaker could as easily meet his end at an impromptu necktie party as be convicted in a court of law. Fingerprint matching and DNA databases were nonexistent. My own cousin Red John Dunn capped off a ten-year enlistment with the Texas Rangers under Captain Bland Chamberlain and later Captain Leander McNelly, with several instances of involvement with vigilante justice. Taking the law into one's own hands was expeditious but illegal and fraught with far too many instances of innocent men being on the wrong end of a rope or bullet. Dunn himself was tried twice for murder and acquitted both times.

With *The Black Gold Mob: Capping a Crime Gusher,* I'm right pleased to share my story of building upon my legendary father's lawman footsteps and seeking to make significant headway in bringing justice to Texas. Blood, as shed by both innocent and evil men, colors the Strip. Desperate killers, rustlers, disease, and savages are part and parcel to my life. Just about anywhere I ride, death could be reaching for my reins. While it could be said that I emulate my father in building considerable notoriety and creating enemies by virtue of my success in bringing lawbreakers to justice, I am very much my own man and have begun to establish reliable allies.

While the "Cast of Historical Characters" provides some helpful true-to-life framework to the life and times in Texas, woven into *The Black Gold Mob: Capping a Crime Gusher* are actual settlers as drawn from my own Irish ancestors committed to taming the frontier. Such real-life characters, coupled with actual events, have served to reinforce the fictional setting with a strong dose of historical reality.

For anyone of a mind that the frontier had been won, they had a second think coming. The wild prairies and hills of Texas were alive and kicking, lawbreaking was very much in abundance, and what one might call the residuals of old wild west justice prevailed. It's in this setting that the need for justice remained strong for better or worse.

Kindly,
Lucas Dunn Jr.

THE BLACK GOLD MOB

PROLOGUE

I HAD RIDDEN out of Corpus Christi at a canter. There was no point in delaying the seeming inevitability of being shot at. Where might a bushwhacker lurk? Thoughts of Gordon Murphy and the Irish Mob shot through my brain. I hadn't gone far when my old friend Buffalo Watts caught up with me. He'd visited Heaven's Gate Ranch and found it under siege. A shamrock had been pinned to the barn door.

We decided not to approach the ranch through the archway, but come in from the south. We split up.

Clumsy was an understatement as far as Murphy's hired guns were concerned. There were three of them hidden in an arroyo that ran along the lane from the gateway arch to the big house. I wondered whether they realized that they weren't on a payroll anymore. No matter for the present. I motioned to Watts to circle around. We'd get the bushwhackers in a sort of crossfire from behind them.

I stalked to within about twenty feet of the three. The first thing they heard was me levering a round into the chamber of my Winchester. "Y'all can drop those guns and raise your hands. You're under arrest."

Taken fully by surprise, they turned in unison with mouths gaping. The tallest of the trio pointed his carbine in my direction, but my finger was far faster than his. A hole appeared where his nose had been. He'd become a dead man standing.

The other two were considering their options when they heard Watts off to their left as he pulled back the hammer on his rifle. The two dropped their rifles.

"Keep them in your sights, Buffalo," I said as I strode forward with manacles. As I began to cuff the two of them together, I heard a voice from the direction of the big house.

"Let 'em go, Dunn, you sonofabitch, or I'll kill your family."

Watts and I froze. That cowardly, lily-livered skunk Kyle McClintock was holding my family hostage.

I clobbered both gunmen up the side of their heads. When they came to, they might leave, but they would be manacled together.

"The man who was paying you is gone, McClintock. It's over. Let my family go." I tentatively walked toward the house. I could see Cassie. Her hands were tied up high to a gallery support with Sean and Bode seated beside her, crying with fear. McClintock just behind Cassie.

"Drop your gun, Junior. This ain't about railroads."

This was personal. Kyle McClintock had never forgiven me for winning Cassie's favor years back. There was no standoff at play here. Either McClintock or I was going to die. I laid my Winchester on the ground.

Cassie looked fearless, but I knew she was scared.

I locked eyes with Cassie. I strove to let her know that I'd save her.

McClintock smiled at me as he ran his hand up Cassie's body and grabbed a breast. "Come on, Junior." He taunted as he motioned me to head toward him.

ONE
MURDERING SKUNK

MCCLINTOCK'S SMILE would have made the Devil himself envious. He stroked Cassie's breast again and then undid the top buttons. "She be mine now, Dunn! Your daddy ain't around to help you."

I saw Buffalo Watts slightly behind me and off to my right. I wondered where our hired ranch hands were? I reckoned they were likely off on some far pasture out of sight and earshot. The two thugs we'd knocked out were already coming to. I stood there feeling naked and vulnerable with my Winchester lying in the dirt. "What now, McClintock?" I challenged.

He chambered a round and fired close to my feet.

Watts raised his Sharps with the hammer drawn back.

McClintock never missed a beat. He swung his rifle and blew a hole through Watts's shoulder.

Watts fell with a gasp. "Damn!" he groaned.

"You're a coward, McClintock!" I responded.

The man smiled and unfastened two more buttons on Cassie's dress. A tad too much flesh for public viewing was now revealed. "You unbuckle that gun belt, Junior, and drop it to the ground real easy like."

I could hear Watts groaning. I sighed and let my gun belt drop. I gave McClintock a questioning look.

"You can drop that badge, Junior. I'm not killing no badge-carrying lawman." McClintock's triangular, snake-like face made the serpent in the Garden of Eden look innocent. There was no tempting here; just cowardly taunting.

"What are you waiting for?" I pressed. Inside, I was trembling. Could I reach my gun and shoot the man and not hit Cassie or my boys?

"I know what you're thinking, Junior. Go ahead and try it."

The tension was unbearable. Tears streamed down Cassie's face.

McClintock tore open the front of her dress. He kissed a breast while keeping his rifle pointed at me. "Damn, they be sweet, Junior," he leered. "Nice and firm."

Anger welled up inside me, but I had to remain in control of my senses.

The two hired henchmen staggered to the bottom step of the gallery. They were still manacled together.

"Fetch the damned key, you idiots!" ordered McClintock as he stroked Cassie's bare breasts tauntingly.

Just maybe, my chance to save Cassie was about to arrive.

I got to wondering where Brody and Tess were. They were young, but not serving in their intended roles as defenders of our home. If I survived this, I vowed to train that pair.

Sean and Bode were sobbing and cowering with fear at the end of the gallery.

"Come on, Hal," said one of the hired guns as he pulled his companion toward me. "Where's the damn key?" he sneered.

I swung my hip toward him, as if to say the key was in a pocket. As he stepped to within arm's length of me, I whipped my Bowie knife from behind my back and wrapped my other arm around the man's neck. The point of my knife was at his throat.

The second thug was involuntarily dragged into the fray by virtue of the manacles.

McClintock fired. His bullet plowed through the second thug and lodged in the chest of the one I was choking. As they fell, I dove for my Smith & Wesson.

McClintock aimed at me and squeezed his trigger, but his rifle jammed.

I couldn't shoot for fear of hitting Cassie or the boys.

McClintock shot me an evil grin and dove from the gallery. He leaped onto his horse and spurred away.

I ran after him to try to get off a clean shot to no avail. With a helpless sigh, I turned and rushed up the gallery steps to free Cassie. We hugged for a moment, but she pointed to Watts, groveling with pain in the dirt. We went to his side.

"Come on, pard. Let's get you inside."

"I...I dunno, Lucas. It be purty bad." He was growing paler by the moment. "I think I be losin' blood inside." With that, he coughed up a frothy mix.

"No, Buffalo. Keep breathing. We'll fix you up," I insisted. We got him to the cool of the shade cast by the house. I stuffed my bandana into his wound.

Cassie was in tears. She knew that Watts went way back with our family. The mountain man had survived bears, cougars, wolves, Indians, and bandits, He'd hunted with us, and hung around to watch our backsides.

"Wagh," he whispered. "Ne'er told yuhs, but I love y'all," he rasped. He coughed once more and breathed his last. The wrinkles in his bearded, sun-weathered face began to smooth out as all tension left his body. He lay at peace.

I was overcome with grief, cradling his head and trembling with great sobs. "Why?" I hollered to the sky. "Why?" I cradled my friend's head. "Why?" I whispered. The Good Book might say that vengeance makes for a hollow victory, but Kyle McClintock was going to die at my hands.

Cassie clung to me. The boys sensed safety and came running, then pulled back at the sight of Watts and the two dead hired guns. Brody and Tess finally appeared but hung back.

"Let's go inside," I urged. We needed to deal as a family with this terrible mix of emotions. Burying Watts and disposing of the two gunmen could wait a little while. I reckoned it would yet be a couple of hours before our ranch hands rode in. I also needed to get word of Buffalo's demise to my dad. Cassie's folks would want to know as well, though we'd spare them the details of her ordeal at McClintock's slimy hands.

McClintock? The craven coward was long gone for now.

I awakened Cassie with a gentle nudge. "I'll get us some coffee," I said, swinging my legs to the floor and pulling on my pants. I shook out my boots and slipped them on. There were no hidden critters.

Cassie looked at me through sleepy eyes. She knew that her man getting up to fetch coffee could only mean that he had something serious to discuss. She turned to her side, half-tempted to close her eyelids and drift back to slumberland. She heard the dogs bark excitedly, as I let them out. Sean and Bode were still asleep.

I tiptoed up the stairs with a hot coffee in each hand. The aroma of the dark brew lifted my spirits. I walked into our bedroom, shut the door gently with my foot, and placed Cassie's coffee on the nightstand beside her. I took a sip of mine before setting it down. It was strong enough to turn a spoon into molten metal. I sat beside Cassie and swung my still booted legs up and crossed them.

Cassie looked up expectantly from her pillow. "Just say it," she whispered.

"Say what?" I responded.

"You're going to hunt him down."

There was no slipping secrets past my beloved wife. I nodded.

"You going to clear it with Captain Hughes?"

"Expect I ought to," I said gravely. This would be serious business.

"What about Sheriff McTiernan?" she pressed.

I sighed. "I suppose he ought to know. It's his jurisdiction," I reluctantly admitted.

Cassie took a sip of coffee and spat it out with a gasp. "What is this?" she exclaimed.

"Too strong?" I teased.

"Let me make it the next time."

I smiled. I preferred her brewing it anyway.

"Are you looking for my permission to hunt McClintock?" she asked. She'd already awakened each of the past two nights with nightmares. Her gazed deeply into my eyes. "I'd dearly like to shoot his sorry…" She let the sentiment hang.

Sean peeked into our bedroom. "Hi, Dad, hi, Momma," came his tentative young voice.

Cassie smiled. "Go wake Bode and meet us downstairs for breakfast," she said lovingly.

TWO
HUNTING A KILLER?

IT WAS SETTLED. I think the fact that McClintock had made it personal by attacking her made the decision to support my pursuit a tad easier for Cassie. To make it official, I had been cleared by Captain Hughes to hunt down the killer hired by the evil bunch that had sought to control the railroads. He appreciated that McClintock had threatened my family. I had also taken a ride into Corpus Christi to let Sheriff McTiernan know what I was up to. The sheriff even managed to get the government folks to put up a thousand-dollar reward—dead or alive. I reckoned that I would be able to hunt my prey quite legal-like. Whether I'd bring McClintock in dead or alive remained to be seen.

In the inner recesses of my mind, I had to deal with a message from Captain Hughes to call him after I'd dealt with McClintock. It seemed that another case awaited me. I was flattered. However, it gnawed at me a bit at a time when I needed to focus on my immediate task. I'd given quite a bit of thought as to where to begin my hunt. Where might my prey be lurking? A lot of folks between Corpus Christi and San Antonio knew me on sight. Could the same be said for McClintock? My gut told me that my prey would head to familiar territory, and that would place him somewhere in the vicinity of Nuecestown.

The morning of my departure arrived crisp and warm with clear blue skies stretching from horizon to horizon. I stood hat in hand over Buffalo Watts's grave. I found myself nearly as distraught over the loss of my good friend Buffalo Watts as I had years back at the killing of my younger brother at the hands of a murderous rustler. Watts had been considered like family. So it was that I spent a few moments at Watts's grave before heading out to track down Kyle McClintock.

I'd curried Tornado a bit more than usual this particular morning. My big Appaloosa stallion pranced nervously in anticipation of whatever adventure I must have in store for him. The dogs must have sensed what I was up to, as they yipped and cavorted about. At breakfast, Sean and Bode hung on to me as though not wanting me to leave. Cassie dealt with her nerves by clanking dishes in the sink. The tensions were palpable.

I wondered what Kyle McClintock must have been thinking. It went without saying that I'd come after him. He had to be half scared to death of what I might do to him. This went far beyond any schoolyard fight we had as kids. He'd threatened my family and tried to kill me. Would he leave the territory or lie in wait like the coward he was to bushwhack me?

The best thing to be said for my departure was that Cassie made it memorable in our bed the night before. Last night had been no exception.

Goodbyes were never easy, and they grew tougher as my boys grew older.

I rode easy like into Nuecestown. The town was showing its age, and hopes for renewal hung on having a railroad pass through. A snub by the railroad would serve as a death knell. It would only be a matter of time before the town faded away. I shook my head as we shuffled past places that now lived in memories. Doc's house was run down, reflective of his passing. The boarding house was a tad shabby, and the meat packing plant had become a vermin-infested, rusting hulk. Even Tornado seemed to sense the old town's imminent demise.

Nevertheless, folks strove to keep the place alive. The ferry still operated, and ground had been broken for a new restaurant. The jailhouse was as decrepit as ever. I recalled my dad telling me of his reluctance to leave prisoners there for fear of escape. Sheriff McTiernan didn't seem especially inclined to make necessary upgrades.

I headed for the ferry, figuring that most anybody passing through would use it to cross the Nueces River. The ferryman was like a history book, seemingly able to recall years of names and faces with unfathomable ease. Of course, he'd spent years ferrying folks across the brownish river waters meandering by. Many an outlaw had passed Pete Driscoll's eyes. His ferry bore the scars of a few gun battles as well.

As I approached the ferry landing, I snuck a final glance over my shoulder at the town. I dismounted from Tornado and walked over to the ferryman. Old Pete Driscoll was lounging on a rickety old chair, picking at his teeth with a long grass stem. "Howdy, Pete," I hailed.

Driscoll didn't look up. "Saw yuh comin', Junior. Yuh headed across or somethin' else on yer mind?"

The old fellow didn't miss much. "Looking for Kyle McClintock," I ventured.

"Still wearin' the badge like yer daddy, eh?"

"Yep," I responded.

"Yer friend McClintock passed through couple days back. Sonofabitch nearly got away without payin'. Old Bessy convinced him otherwise."

Old Bessy was the ten-gauge shotgun Driscoll kept handy for scoundrels like McClintock. "Did he say where he was headed?"

Driscoll shrugged and chuckled. "Drove me nuts. Blabbered about headin' to Kerrville. Him sayin' how purty it was."

I wish my prey had been heading north or east, where the land was flatter and there were fewer places for ambush cover. The hill country would be a challenge thanks to its hills, ravines, meandering arroyos, mesquite, cactus, and tree mottes. It was a bushwhacker's paradise. I flipped Driscoll a silver dollar. "Thanks kindly, old friend."

"Yuh ain't crossin'?" queried the old ferryman.

I shook my head. "Not today, Pete. I reckon to stay south of the river." If McClintock had crossed and was headed to Kerrville or Fredericksburg, I figured to stay well south of him. He surely knew I'd be hunting him, and there was no point in my making ambush easy.

Driscoll nodded.

We made a brief small talk about my dad and my own growing family before I bid farewell. I reckoned I'd fortified him with enough goings on to make knowledgeable small talk with passersby.

I turned Tornado eastward, thinking on how not so long ago I'd twice foiled bushwhacking attempts by Garth Jones in the Texas hills. There's little to match the satisfaction of sneaking up on someone planning to ambush you. Nevertheless, I dared not underestimate Kyle McClintock. A whinny from Tornado broke my brief meditation. We sidestepped around a rattlesnake.

I decided to take the SA&AP railroad to Kerrville. It would save about ten days of travel time, though I'd miss the old days of riding the Pinta Trail. It would also avoid having to get used to days in the saddle. I might even wind up ahead of McClintock.

So far, so good. The train ride went smoothly, and Tornado endured being boxed into a railcar. He was a happy horse when we disembarked at the Kerrville depot.

Professional courtesy dictated that I pay a visit to Sheriff Vann. This was his jurisdiction. If I were to do any arresting or killing, I'd involve him during or after, depending on the circumstances. I reckoned he remained indebted to me for my having solved those killings on the Guadalupe River a while back.

Once I got Tornado saddled up, I made the short ride from the depot to Vann's office.

"Sheriff?" I declared as I simultaneously knocked and pushed open the door to the sheriff's office.

Vann nearly jumped out of his skin. "Damn it, Dunn! Give a man a chance to respond to your knock!" He leaned down and picked up the papers he'd thrown up in the air with surprise.

"Sorry, John," I apologized while plopping myself in the chair facing his desk.

Vann shoved a paper at me. "You looking for this fellow?" It was a brand spanking new wanted poster sporting the three-thousand-dollar reward for the capture of Kyle McClintock, dead or alive.

I nodded.

"He's not here," said Vann resignedly.

"What do you mean?" I asked.

Vann sighed. "I knew him from years back, when his father used to mosey up here to ship alpaca. I hadn't yet received the sheet on him, though I'm not surprised he'd found trouble."

"So, what happened?" I pressed. I wondered what would send McClintock packing.

"I caught up with him yesterday at the telegraph office in the train depot. We chatted about the weather and his folks while he awaited a reply." Vann leaned forward toward me. "Well, he got his reply. His eyes grew wide, and he lit out on his horse like his tail was on fire."

"Did the telegrapher say what it was about?"

"Like I said, I had no papers and no right to pry," said Vann regrettably.

"Well, I expect we ought to pay the telegraph office a visit," I suggested.

"Go ahead, Lucas. It's your case, and I reckon he's long gone from Kerr County," Vann said while handing the poster to me.

I thanked the sheriff and headed pronto back to the depot. Tornado was likely wondering about my strange behavior. I'm sure a stall with oats and hay was on his mind.

"May I help you?" asked the telegrapher as I approached his window.

"I'm Texas Ranger Lucas Dunn. I'm pursuing this man." I showed him the wanted circular on McClintock. "Sheriff Vann says that he witnessed this fugitive sending and receiving a message yesterday. Do you recall the message?"

"I…I don't believe I can share private messages, Ranger Dunn," stammered the telegrapher.

I thought on his response. I reckoned I could find a judge and get an order, but speed was of the essence. "How about just telling me who he communicated with?" I nonchalantly slipped a silver dollar onto the counter.

The telegrapher looked offended that I was attempting to bribe him, then gave a devious sort of smile. "A fellow named Gordon Murphy in New York City." He snatched the silver dollar.

The answer stunned me. I nearly blurted out Irish Mob. "Thanks kindly," I said to the telegrapher and slid another silver dollar toward him. He had no idea how valuable he'd been.

It sounded as though Gordon Murphy was calling in his hired guns. Something was afoot. The man's previous efforts had been based out of Dallas, and it seemed unlikely that the leopard would change its spots. My first task would be to get in touch with Captain Hughes.

Poor Tornado endured another ride to the sheriff's office. I figured that I owed it to Vann to tell him what I'd learned. I rode up and climbed from my saddle. I knocked and waited.

"Come on in, Dunn," called out Vann.

I stepped on in. "How'd you know?"

"Got eyes and a window," he responded with a grin. He'd made his point.

I chuckled and grabbed my usual seat. "Well, Sheriff, Kyle McClintock lit out because he received a call from a higher power."

"God?"

I rolled my eyes. "Not hardly. The Irish Mob is back or planning to come back."

"What are you going to do?" asked Vann.

"I haven't talked with Captain Hughes yet. I have a

feeling that the US Marshals will be turned on to this case." I replied.

"What about McClintock? Queried the sheriff.

"Humph! He's little more than a flea on the dog. Make no mistake, I'd like to bag him for what he did to me and my family, not to mention murdering a family friend."

"But?" asked Vann.

"I have to get my priorities in order. Make no mistake, Sheriff; if I catch McClintock..." I left my words hanging.

"I'll always do what I can, Dunn," was Vann's sincere reply. "Thanks for letting me know."

With that, I bade goodbye and headed to the hotel to gather my thoughts on how best to approach Captain Hughes.

For now, it was looking like hunting a killer was no longer my top priority.

THREE
JURISDICTION

CAPTAIN HUGHES ADVISED me to sit tight while he checked with Governor Culberson. He suspected that this would be a federal matter, but reckoned that I'd work with the US Marshals thanks to my history with Gordon Murphy. Hughes had heard that the Irish Mob had made inroads up in some big cities and were of a vengeful spirit at my having disrupted their Dallas plans. To me, that translated into watching my backside.

I sat in my hotel room and penciled a note to telegraph to Cassie. I tore it up. Better to find a telephone.

The telephone operator was a family acquaintance and a tad chatty but finally put me through to Cassie. The phone seemed to ring for an eternity.

"No one's answering, Mr. Dunn," said the operator.

"Try again, please," I insisted. It was midday, and Cassie had a lot of chores to tackle each day. Maybe Sean or Bode were needing attention or the dogs.

The operator gave a few more rings.

"Hello?" Cassie's voice finally came through. She

sounded annoyed, as though she was fearing a call from one of her gossipy friends.

"Go ahead, Mr. Dunn," squeaked the operator's voice.

"Sweetheart?" I ventured.

"Oh, but it's good to hear your voice. It's been a crazy day, Lucas. Zach Wilson's been out to fix a leak in the cistern, and that crazy mare got loose from the corral and…" She paused. "Where are you?"

"Still in Kerrville. I'm waiting to hear from Captain Hughes."

"What of McClintock?" Cassie asked.

"He's headed to Dallas to join up with you know what." I dared not mention the Irish Mob, as the operator was likely listening.

Cassie caught my drift. "Are you saying it's back?"

"Looks to be," I replied. "Whatever the captain says, I reckon to get home before heading out to tackle it."

Cassie still had dreams of McClintock's assault. "You still on the hunt?" she pressed.

"Yes, but I'll talk more when I get home."

"Hi, Daddy!" Sean piped up into the telephone. He was talking now.

"I'll be home soon, son," I assured him. "I have to go, Cassie."

"Love you, Lucas," she said as she wrestled the telephone from Sean.

"Love you, too." I hung up. This was the sort of moment that caused me to doubt my being a lawman. If only we could create more income from Heaven's Gate Ranch, I could bury the badge for good. I suspected my dad dealt with this dilemma most every day.

A knock at the door interrupted my musings. With a hand on the Smith & Wesson in my holster, I cracked open the door.

"Telegram, sir," said the young boy handing it to me.

"Thanks, son," I responded and placed a nickel in his outstretched paw.

He took off with a smile.

I grabbed a seat and unfolded the telegram.

TEXAS RANGER LUCAS DUNN, JR
FRONTIER BATTALION
KERRVILLE, TX

CONTACT US MARSHAL MILLER IN DALLAS TX. EXPECTING COOP.

TWO WEEKS LEAVE APPROVED.
REWARD STANDS FOR MCCORMICK.

TEXAS RANGER CAPTAIN JOHN HUGHES
FRONTIER BATTALION
BROWNSVILLE TX

Well, that settled the near future. I reckoned to pack my gear and head back to Nuecestown and Heaven's Gate Ranch.

I figured to stop by and bid farewell to Sheriff Vann as a courtesy before heading to the railroad depot. It was a right pretty day, so I decided to walk Tornado over to the sheriff's office.

I likely hadn't gone more than a dozen steps from the stable behind the boarding house when an unfamiliar voice froze me.

"Yuh thet damned Ranger done kilt my frens?" came slurred mutterings.

I turned to see a grizzled, half-drunk man in sweat-stained clothes staggering toward me. Of special concern was the Colt .45 Peacemaker that the man was waving around. "Whoa, partner. You must be mistaken." I tried to defuse the situation.

"Nah, twas you. Yuh kilt 'em back in Skidmore," he insisted with a belch. The waving of his gun began to slow as he tried to aim it at me.

My hand was a long way from the Smith & Wesson on my hip. I dropped Tornado's reins and gave him a nudge out of any possible line of fire. I could smell the whiskey on the man's breath. To understate, this was a serious situation.

In the midst of figuring what to do and hoping the drunk didn't accidentally pull the trigger, Sheriff Vann turned the corner behind the man.

"Burt Toliver, what the tarnation do you think you're doing?" challenged Vann.

The man he'd called Toliver stopped, grabbed his belly, and threw up. He wiped his mouth with his sleeve and was about to address Vann, when the sheriff neatly relieved him of the gun.

"Let's go take a walk, Burt," urged Vann.

"B-b-but this man kilt my frens," Toliver insisted.

"Come along peacefully, Burt. Let's not be making a fuss." Vann took a strong grip of the man's arm. "Sorry, Ranger, he gets ornery when he's had a few too many."

"Appreciate you showing up, Sheriff. I was headed your way to tell you I'd heard from Captain Hughes and will be heading out. I appreciate your hospitality…and your excellent timing."

Vann smiled. "Pleasant travels, Ranger Dunn. Stop by anytime." He was about to lead Toliver away to sleep off his drunk, when he paused. "Have you heard?"

"Heard what?" I was anxious to get to the depot but paused.

"Remember back earlier this year when the cruiser USS Maine was blown up in the harbor in Havana, Cuba?" It was sort of a rhetorical question, as pretty much everyone knew of the incident. "Well, that fellow Theodore Roosevelt, the one who was training troops down in San Antonio, led his Rough Riders up San Juan Hill and made quite a name for himself. He's a man to watch, Ranger Dunn. Mark my words." He began to lead Toliver away but stopped again. "Oh, and the Spanish fleet got wiped out at some godforsaken place called the Philippines. We sure put a whipping on the Spanish."

"That's great news, Sheriff." I turned to go. I wasn't quite sure how a Spanish-American War would affect me, but good news was welcome. I'd heard a thing or two about Roosevelt, but nothing that stuck with me. I recalled that one of my cousins had considered joining the Rough Riders, but he decided it wouldn't be exciting enough. Apparently, he'd misjudged.

"Yep. That man Roosevelt is going places," advised Vann. "Safe travels, Ranger Dunn." He dragged a stumbling Toliver away.

I tipped my hat to Vann and led Tornado toward the depot. Soon enough, he'd be cavorting with his mares, and I'd be tightening ties with my growing family. My time would be limited, but I'd use all I could. I'd come to realize how precious a commodity time was.

FOUR
PRECIOUS TIME

THE TRAIN TRIP from Kerrville was uneventful. As I rode home from the depot in Corpus Christi, I realized that I was experiencing an inner peace in not worrying about Kyle McClintock. I knew I'd eventually have to confront him, but I reckoned that, for now, he'd be kept busy up in Dallas. I didn't feature taking on the Irish Mob again and was concerned about how cooperative the US Marshals would be. I patted Tornado's neck as much to be affectionate as to find comfort in my loyal steed.

I rode Tornado up to the archway gate and reined in. I took a long look at the letters on the arch that spelled out Heaven's Gate Ranch. Why did I suddenly feel a sense of foreboding sweep over me? "Do you feel it, Tornado?" I said aloud. He answered with a snort, whinny, and bob of his head.

As I rode up to the house, Cassie was loading a basket and the boys into the buckboard. The dogs, Brody and Tess, had already jumped into the bed of the wagon. "Where y'all headed?" I hailed.

"Lucas! You're home. Praise the Lord!" She dropped the boys in the buckboard and ran to greet me.

I slid from my saddle and caught her in my arms. "Oh, Lucas. Your dad's real sick."

I stepped back. "Dad's sick?"

"Your mom says he caught some terrible fever. It's burning him up. I was about to head over to help."

"I...I'll ride with you." I put aside all other thoughts as mere distractions and tied Tornado behind the buckboard. I boosted Cassie onto the seat and climbed up myself, grabbing the reins as I sat. I gave a chuck to the team, and we headed out.

Roiling through my mind were thoughts of my bigger-than-life, seemingly-immortal father, struck down by a fever. He'd taken bullets that nearly killed him, but this was an unseen threat.

We pulled up in front of my folks' house. I paused to take in the place. While they had spent the past ten years overseeing ranch holdings that were better than three times the size of Heaven's Gate, they lived in a modest single-story home built of Texas limestone with a Spanish-tile red roof. Humble for sure. Dad and Mom were more concerned with giving of their wealth to the community and church than spending lavishly on themselves. Plus, they had always been willing and able to help us kids during hard times. Their generosity helped them to be able to enjoy fifteen grandchildren. Thus, it was no surprise that a couple of my brothers and a sister had arrived ahead of us.

While Cassie ushered Sean and Bode inside, I saw to the team. The dogs followed me to the barn, nipping at the heels of Tornado and the two geldings that had pulled the buckboard.

With the horses properly settled, I sucked up my courage and headed for the house. I opened the great carved mahogany door to be greeted by a heavy silence. I greeted my siblings while looking around for Cassie. "How's Dad?" I asked my brother Johnny.

He said not a word but nodded his head toward the bedroom. I spotted my mom standing in the doorway, looking in on Cassie as she stood by my dad's bed. Mom saw me and motioned me over.

"What's happened, Mom?" I asked.

"Yellow fever, Lucas."

"But…I thought it…" I groped for words.

"It's not been eradicated, son. Your dad's fever came on a couple of days ago. The doc is at a loss to help." She wiped tears from her eyes and buried her face in my chest. "He's burning up, Lucas."

I'd heard stories of friends and family members who had survived the yellow fever, but knew some had passed away. I'd heard that about thirty years back, Corpus Christi had lost better than ten percent of its citizens to the disease, including five Dunn adults and children. I hugged Mom and joined Cassie at my dad's bedside. I was shocked at what I saw. His skin was yellow. I'd heard that meant his liver was under attack. The once vibrant eyes stared off into space. The evil end that desperado's bullets had failed to accomplish was bringing down the legend that was my dad.

Cassie turned to me and nestled her face against my shoulder. Like my mom, she'd been wiping tears.

"Never seen Dad like this," I whispered.

At the sound of my voice, a flicker of life appeared in my dad's eyes. He turned his head ever-so-slowly toward me. "L...love you, son," he murmured. He took a struggling breath.

My mom walked in and stood beside me. She took Dad's hand in hers.

Dad's eyes riveted on mine. "Take care of your mom. Ranch be yours." With his free hand, he slowly drew out an often-folded, yellowed piece of paper from beneath the sheet. His eyes motioned for me to take it.

I took the paper and unfolded it. It was his last will and testament. I read it slowly, glancing at Dad between sentences.

He now wore a peaceful, satisfied expression.

I took a deep breath and continued reading. The will gave me the ranch, but I was to compensate my brothers and sisters and support my mom living out her years in this house he'd built for her. There wasn't anything else to it. I kissed my dad on his forehead. "I love you, too, Dad." I handed the will to my mom.

The rest of the family was watching from the doorway. Sensing that Dad was close to coming to the end of his life's journey, I motioned them to enter the room. Ever-so-solemnly, they gathered around the bed.

Dad's rheumy eyes scanned the gathered family, pausing at each of us as though taking in some wondrous never-to-be-forgotten sight. A smile creased his lips. I saw him squeeze Mom's hand as he breathed his last.

Sobs swept the room. Two of my older brothers shifted uncomfortably, not knowing quite how to handle their grief. Mom collapsed onto the bed beside her lifelong love.

Cassie buried her face in my chest and wept inconsolably.

I felt the tears well up in the corner of my eye, but, as I scanned the room, I realized that, despite being the youngest, I would be the one they'd be turning to in this time of grief. I had to be the rock upon which they'd lean. I was every bit my father's son. I simply stood with my arm around Cassie and grieved silently. I appreciated my fortune to have arrived from my Kerrville trip in time to see my dad alive one last time. I reflexively patted the will now residing in my pocket.

Funerals didn't necessarily happen overnight. There were a few things to arrange. It would take a couple of days to prepare for a proper burial.

The Dunn family plot lay behind our house at Heaven's Gate Ranch. There, on a knoll overlooking the ranch, were the graves of our immediate ancestors. Brothers, sisters, and my mom's folks took their eternal rest at the spot. The bullets Mom used to kill the man who'd murdered my younger brother still lay spread across his grave. Beautiful bluebonnets grew in the little plot.

We had a fine mahogany box built in which to rest my dad's bones for eternity. We reckoned Saint Peter would welcome his soul through the Pearly Gates. My dad was never one for fancy events, so the funeral would be simple. He'd have wanted it so.

My dad had lived a full life, from Irish immigrant to lawman and rancher. He'd married for love and helped Elisa raise their eleven children. Dad had faced death and had nearly been killed. He'd built a legendary reputation as a Texas Ranger admired by all. He realized that time was a precious commodity, so he made the most of his life on this earth.

Dad's interment was a private affair, as family gathered around. I wished Dad's old friend One Arrow could have made the long journey from the reservation. Young children

—the future of the Dunn clan—played around, no doubt oblivious to the proceedings. The women dabbed eyes and noses with handkerchiefs as I delivered a eulogy. As Dad's box was lowered into the ground, the sobbing increased.

My mom had already pretty-much cried herself out the night before. Cassie and I had sat with her, offering what comfort we could.

"After Lucas is buried, Junior," she said. "After he's in the ground, I think we need to celebrate his life. He'd want us to remember the joys, the good times."

I wasn't quite sure what she meant.

"Invite everyone back to the house. Open some wine, lay out a spread, play some music, and everyone remember Luke's accomplishments."

We all headed back to Mom's house, and everyone pitched in to create a celebration of Dad's life. The air became filled with the stories—most of them seriously embellished—of my dad.

Night descended on the gathering, yet the house was lit up like a Christmas tree. I was talking with one of my brothers-in-law when the front door swung open. I did a double-take. Standing with hat in hand was Texas Ranger Captain John Hughes. He nodded my way, then scanned the room to pick out my mom. Before I could make a move toward him, he'd begun to walk over to my mom.

"Mrs. Dunn, ma'am," he began.

My mom looked up at Hughes with a curious expression. She hadn't a clue as to who he was.

"Begging your pardon, Mrs. Dunn. I'm Captain Hughes of your son Junior's company. I've come to express my deepest condolences. Captain Dunn raised a fine son whom you can be proud of." He paused. "But, that's not why I'm here."

Mom looked at him questioningly.

By this time, I had walked over and was joined by Cassie.

Captain Hughes produced a plaque featuring a highly polished Texas Ranger badge. "The Texas Rangers are of a mind to honor your husband. Governor Culberson has authorized a fund in his name to support ailing Rangers, and it's my honor to inform you of it. You will also receive an annual stipend as a token of appreciation for his service to Texas."

The generosity of the Texas Rangers took me by surprise, but I was especially touched by the fact that Captain Hughes had requested the honor of delivering the news.

My mom was deeply grateful. "Captain, thank you ever so kindly. Please do join our celebration of Luke's life."

The celebration continued well into the night. The morning would find many celebrants sleeping about the house.

☆☆

Captain Hughes and I commiserated a bit over breakfast about the Irish Mob. He'd taken our offer to spend the night at our house at Heaven's Gate. While chewing on a generous slice of bacon, he shared what he knew of Deputy US Marshal Miller.

"Bill Miller's a tough customer, Junior. You're going to have your hands full, as he likes to be in total control." Hughes took a long sip of coffee.

"Not a listener?" I ventured.

"You'll have to find your voice with him. When you have an opinion, be ready to defend it." He emptied his cup.

Cassie undred and padded over and refilled it.

"Thanks kindly, Mrs. Dunn," said Hughes. "I must say, those were the finest bear sign I've ever had the pleasure to enjoy."

Cassie smiled. "Looks as though the passing of my husband's father has put us in a bit of a dilemma, Captain."

This caught Hughes off guard and fully surprised me. With all the post-funeral goings-on, I hadn't given any particular thought to the future. "Dilemma?" I asked.

"We're looking at handling some fifty thousand acres, Captain. Lucas here is responsible for all of it. It's going to be a stretch to be a Texas Ranger and run a ranch of this size." There, she'd said what had been festering in her mind all night and into this morning. Why should her husband risk his life as a lawman when he had a profitable ranch and loving family to care for?

Hughes nearly choked on the slug of coffee he was about to take. He gazed questioningly at me.

"Er...I really hadn't given it any thought." I looked furtively at Cassie, then to Hughes and back to Cassie.

There was a hint of triumph in Cassie's eyes, as she picked up the empty plates from the table. "Care for more coffee, Lucas, sweetheart?" She smiled mischievously and headed to the kitchen sink to dump the dishes and grab the nearby coffee pot.

"Can I count on you for this Dallas business?" asked Hughes.

"Seems Cassie and I have some discussing to do," I responded. I caught her smile in my peripheral vision.

Hughes sighed and took a sip of coffee. "Well, I gave you a couple of weeks, Junior. Take a month if you need it to make the best decision for you," he paused. "and your conscience." He gave an understanding look to Cassie. "Do what's right. I don't think time is necessarily critical," he added and drained his coffee cup.

"Thanks, Captain. Cassie and I will talk about it."

"Well, I'd best be on my way. You know where to reach me, Ranger Dunn. Thanks again for your hospitality, and my condolences once again on your loss."

I stood deep in thought atop the hill, looking down at the freshly covered grave. Flower petals were still strewn around. Turning and looking out over the rolling landscape, it was impossible to not appreciate the ranch that lay before me. I'd left the house right after the captain's departure and now stood mustering my thoughts as to what the future held. There was no avoiding taking this up with Cassie. I turned my gaze back down at my dad's grave. "What would you do, Dad?" I murmured.

"He'd tell you to do what is right, Lucas." Mom had slipped in beside me while I was deep in thought. "You must do what's right and in your heart, son," she counseled. "But…Cassie must be part of the decision. Whatever you do, be sure she's in agreement."

Mom was right. I sighed and gave her a hug. I looked off toward the corral beside the barn. Tornado was prancing about, itching for a ride.

Mom saw straight into what I was thinking. "There's no putting it off, son," she advised. Dang, but my mom was wise.

I kissed her forehead. "Thanks."

"Come visit when you have a chance. I learned your dad's secret ingredient for the brisket."

My eyes grew big as saucers. "You mean?"

She nodded, then chuckled. "You're going to have to step up to the task." The mesquite that was used to smoke the brisket was from a stack of wood saturated with Dad's pee.

I suddenly found myself relaxed and enjoying a bit of a laugh. "Thanks, Mom." I headed back to the house and Cassie. I reckoned to stop by our little wine cellar and fetch a bottle of wine to sweeten our conversation. I still hadn't decided which course to take. I felt a responsibility to Captain Hughes and the Texas Rangers. But—and that was a huge but—time was precious. Time spent being a lawman was time from my loved ones. Last but hardly least, there was a lot of ranch to deal with—fifty thousand sprawling acres of ranch with nearly a thousand beeves, about two hundred horses, and a menagerie of hogs, sheep, goats, and chickens. Hiring someone to serve as foreman was a possibility, but was it fair to place overall responsibility on Cassie?

I was nearly to the house when a tall, lean fellow with a red handlebar mustache flecked with gray and a slouch hat rode up the lane toward me. It was my cousin, Red John Dunn. Red John was sort of the gray sheep of the family. That is, he wasn't quite contrary enough to be the black sheep outcast. He'd ridden with Texas Ranger Captain Bland Chamberlain and then with Captain Warren Wallace, both Texas Ranger leaders of less-than-savory character who did little to uphold the reputation of the force. Red John fit in well with them.

After the Texas Rangers, Red John did some work on the huge King Ranch while mixing in a bit of vigilante activity. He was twice acquitted of murder. He gained fame for helping lead a posse driving off Mexican bandits during the famous Good Friday Raid of 1875 outside Corpus Christi. Red John finally settled as a dairyman, got married, and became a museum curator in his home near Nuecestown. To say the least, Red John had plenty of life experience and advice to offer. As he rode up, I couldn't help but think of Captain Hughes.

"Howdy, Junior," he said with a smile and finger twist of his mustache.

"Welcome, cousin. What brings you to these parts?" I figured to get right to it. I wanted to get the conversation going with Cassie.

"Just passin' through. Hear tell you've got this place under your wings now," he ventured. "You hangin' up the badge?"

"Haven't decided," I responded. I gave him a hard-eyed look.

"No shame in hanging it up. I done it twice." He shifted in his saddle. "Of course, I didn't have any lawman work unfinished." Red John gave a sheepish grin.

"You staying in that saddle?" I pressed.

He shook his head slowly. "Like I said, Junior. Just passin' through. Reckoned to see what you were up to." He still had that smile pasted across his lips.

Red John sure could be an enigma. He'd gotten the Texas Ranger business out of his blood and settled down. Did it still flow in mine? "I'll be sure to let you know, cousin." He'd fertilized the seed of responsibility lingering in me. Captain Hughes wasn't here, but I was pretty sure he'd be sporting a self-satisfied smile.

"If you stay with the badge, I'd be pleased to help out here as needed. I expect Pat would, too…and Nick." He tipped his hat. "Take care, Junior." He turned his horse and trotted back up the lane.

He generously tossed in the names of other cousins, his assurance that the Dunn family would be supportive. Pat Dunn, known as the Duke of Padre Island, raised longhorns on the northern seventy-five miles of the island just outside Corpus Christi, while my cousin Nick Dunn ranched over in nearby Alice. Nick especially appreciated family, as he had eleven children of his own. Both were men of faith and family, as toughened by the trials and tribulations of the gritty vocation of ranching.

In a way, I appreciated Red John's sentiments and offering. I was thinking on it, as I began heading up the stairs to the gallery. My peripheral vision caught something lying beside one of the railing posts. A railroad spike! Where in tarnation had that come from? A slip of paper was wrapped around it and fastened with a piece of rawhide tied in a neat bow. I put aside the wine bottle, picked up the spike, and freed the paper. I unfolded it and read what turned out to be a warning: "STAY HOME OR DIE." Whoever had created the note had cut letters from newspaper headlines and pasted them into the message. Well, this flew in the face of the pressure to pursue the Irish Mob. I reckoned this was Gordon Murphy's doing. He had returned and was smart enough to figure that I'd be looking to build a case against him.

"Who were you talking with?" asked Cassie as I entered our house.

"Red John was passing through," I said, as I placed the bottle of wine on the kitchen table. I strode over to her and gave a kiss.

"Didn't he want to come in for coffee?" She returned my affections.

"Nope. He just wanted to make my life more difficult," I replied.

Cassie nodded. She spied the wine bottle. "Sean and Bode are napping."

It was as good a time as any to get our discussion on the road.

She paused. "What's that in your hand?"

I'd forgotten to leave the danged railroad spike back on the gallery. "Just a railroad spike," I responded.

Cassie laid that *what-aren't-you-telling-me* look on me. I sighed. "Somebody left it on the gallery."

"And?" she persisted.

I chose two wine goblets from the cupboard and strode back over to the kitchen table. "There was a note."

"And?" she asked with an impatient sigh.

"It was just a threat telling me to stay off the case." I tried to be nonchalant as I pulled the cork from the bottle and poured the wine.

"Just a threat?" she repeated. Cassie sensed that the Texas Ranger in me had been riled up, so she knew better than to press too hard. She placed her hand over mine and sipped some wine. "Our grapes get ever sweeter, Lucas," she said by way of changing the subject.

I looked into her expectant eyes. "Red John said he and my cousins would help take care of the ranch, if I took the case Hughes assigned."

"Texas Ranger runs deep in you, husband."

"I so want to be here with you, Cassie. The boys need to grow up with their father present."

"But?" she said rhetorically.

"I feel an obligation to finish the job." There, I'd said it. It was as though a huge burden had been lifted from my shoulders. My Ranger duty, loyalty, and obligation had been gnawing at me.

"I know you do, Lucas. I'm proud of you for it. Your dad was bust-a-button proud of you, too." She took another sip of wine as though fortifying herself. "You must do what you feel most called to do."

"It's not where my heart is," I responded. "It would haunt me to my dying day, if I quit. I'll also eventually have to deal with Kyle McClintock, no matter what decision is reached."

Cassie hunched her shoulders, as a shiver ran up her spine at the mention of McClintock. "I wish…" she let the sentence fall away. She'd already expressed what she'd do to that sorry excuse for manhood if she had the opportunity. She took a deep breath to bring her anger under control. "Guess we've reached our decision, Lucas," said Cassie. Had it been ours? I think the circumstances had made the decision for us. "And I'm proud of you for it." She poured herself more wine. "Just make sure you come back here alive."

"And?" I asked.

"Make this your final assignment."

I nodded. "Sounds fair."

"I love you, Lucas Dunn."

That she had failed to tack *Junior* on the end wasn't missed. With my dad gone, I was the Lucas Dunn of this family now. I looked deep into her eyes. The wine had warmed our insides.

Cassie nodded. "The boys will nap for a while longer."

We headed upstairs to our bedroom.

FIVE
MARSHAL VS. TEXAS RANGER

DEPUTY US MARSHAL William Miller loomed ahead for me, as I boarded the train for Dallas. The past few weeks with Cassie and the kids had given me pause to doubt the decision to fulfill my obligation to Captain Hughes and the people of Texas, but my duty won out. It had to. Poor Tornado was left at home. If I needed a horse, I'd find one up north. Of course, Tornado had plenty of grass, oats, and mares to keep him from being starved and lonely.

We promoted one of our hands, Billy Don Skuggs, to ranch foreman, and my cousins had confirmed their commitments to help look after the ranch. I suppose I felt about as secure as I could as to the welfare of my family while I was away.

I found an empty seat in the first of the two passenger cars. I traveled light, wearing my Smith & Wesson snug in its holster on my hip and carrying saddlebags and my trusty Winchester. The car was nearly filled to capacity, though I had the bench seat to myself, likely owing to my armament. No one stood out among the eighty or so passengers on board, though my Texas Ranger badge did garner a bit of attention from a couple of ladies. One wondered whether I was chasing a lawbreaker. I told her that I'd keep an eye out for any who happened onto the train.

With no passenger the least bit suspicious to be concerned about, I tipped my hat over my eyes, laid back, and caught some shuteye.

Dallas was a bustling town these days with a population exceeding forty thousand. It surely kept Sheriff Bill Moon busy, not to mention the US Marshals. As cities in Texas went, Dallas was as prime a target as any for the Irish Mob to gain a foothold. Railroads had turned the city into a major hub for business and trading. Dallas had been founded at the intersection of a couple of Indian trading traces, so the railroads served to enhance the city's role in commerce. Trade in leather, cotton, and buffalo hides were at the top of the city's business food chain, while oil interests tended to be further to the south and west. The Irish Mob undoubtedly figured to avoid any obvious connection with oil interests by establishing its roots in Dallas. The growing network of railroads served to facilitate the mob's reach.

I checked in at the brand spanking new Union Depot Hotel. Deputy US Marshal Miller had done me the courtesy of reserving a room.

The desk clerk gave me a once-over, his eyes finally coming to rest on my Texas Ranger badge. "That'll be two dollars in advance, sir." The daily hotel rate was high, but the convenient location offset lodger protest. "Bags, sir?" asked the desk clerk.

"Just what I'm carrying," I responded with a glance to

the saddlebags slung over my shoulder. "I reckon to be here a couple of days."

The clerk looked down his nose as though he was doing me a favor by allowing me to stay in the hotel. "Oh, I see."

"Depends on whether I kill someone or they kill me," I said gravely.

The clerk's eyes widened with alarm. "Er, enjoy your room, sir." He passed me a key.

My humor had the desired effect, though the clerk totally missed it. "Oh, where might I find the US Marshal's Office?" I asked. Miller would be expecting me to meet him later.

The clerk was pleased to provide directions, as I expect it gave him a sense of purpose.

My room was well-appointed, the bed providing the temptation to grab a nap before meeting Miller. I decided instead to avail myself of the hotel café before heading over to Miller's office.

I used this time to take stock of my situation. The Irish Mob was surely aware that I had ignored their warning and was on the case. While I remained concerned as to the whereabouts of Kyle McClintock, there was likely more than one hired gun looking to take down any lawmen challenging the Irish Mob's efforts. US MARSHAL WILLIAM MILLER read the gold lettering on the office door. I knocked.

"Who goes?" came an official-sounding reply.

"Texas Ranger Luke Dunn," I replied.

"Enter," came the curt response.

"Here goes," I said under my breath, as I turned the door handle. I stepped into a sparsely decorated waiting room. White walls and dark doorjamb with oak plank floor.

A young man sat shuffling papers behind a weather-beaten old desk. "You the man the Texas Rangers sent to see Marshal Miller?"

"Captain Hughes did send me to help the marshal with a case," I said straight on. I was finding this young toadstool a tad insufferable. I glanced at two rickety old chairs backed against one wall and decided to remain standing. I'd be embarrassed if I broke one.

The young man faked a cough. "Let me see whether he's available to meet with you." As he stood, he seemed to become painfully aware that I was about twice his size and bore the look of a man who meant business. His eyes caught the Smith & Wesson nestled on my hip and couldn't miss my well-burnished Texas Ranger badge. He shuffled awkwardly to the door to Miller's office and knocked softly.

"Is he here?" came a no-nonsense voice from inside.

"Yes, sir, Marshal Miller."

"Well, send him in, dammit," called out Miller impatiently.

"Er, the marshal will see you now, Ranger Dunn," he said respectfully. The clerk swung the door open for me, and I passed on through.

Miller's office was somewhat of a contrast to the waiting room. One wall featured a large, well-stocked bookcase, while two others featured excellent paintings of western scenes, and the fourth was dominated by a large window looking out onto a garden. Miller's desk looked to be made from oak, and all the seating featured leather cushions. All-in-all, it was likely befitting a Deputy US Marshal. The marshal stood and extended his hand. "Welcome to Dallas, Ranger Dunn."

Miller stood just shy of six feet tall and wore a white shirt with a string tie and black pinstriped trousers. I couldn't see his boots but assumed they were appropriate.

A black coat hung on a coat tree near the entry door. We shook hands. "Thanks kindly, Marshal Miller," I responded with a polite smile.

"Grab a seat. Captain Hughes tells me you've dealt with Murphy and his minions. I'm anxious to learn what you know."

Miller was getting right to the point. I saw a pot of coffee over on a nearby credenza.

"Dang, but I'm not much on hospitality." He'd seen my glance at the coffee. "Help yourself, Ranger Dunn."

I strode over and helped myself. I took a sip as I headed back to the chair. It was terrible coffee, but hot and wet. I wasn't sure what to make of Miller just yet, and the coffee gave me a moment to think.

"You can say it," chided Miller with a grin. "My assistant brews it, and it's not fit for human consumption."

It was good to know that Miller had a sense of humor. I proceeded to provide him with an information dump on what I knew of Gordon Murphy and the Irish Mob. I tried not to embellish my role in getting Murphy to leave Texas or my ensuing cat-and-mouse games with Kyle McClintock. In any case, Murphy and the Irish Mob were back and more determined than ever to set up their operations in Texas. Their greed knew no bounds, and the prospect of tapping into black gold was too good to pass up.

Miller rubbed his chin as he thought on what I'd told him.

"I expect they're looking to set up operations here in Dallas and expand southward, Marshal," I concluded.

"You say they were mixed up with the Railroad Commission of Texas. That confirms what I've heard from other sources." The Deputy US Marshal gave me an appraising stare, as though some idea was percolating in his head. "The big railroads are controlled by powerful folks outside of Texas. Why would they go after railroads?"

It was essentially a rhetorical question, but I answered it anyway. "Railroads were the means to an end."

Miller gave me a curious look. "How's that?"

"Oil. Black gold, Marshal." I took a sip of coffee, which I instantly regretted. Whew, but it tasted horrible. "Oil is going to become an economic giant in Texas. It'll be like gold." Thus far, I was finding Miller easy to deal with. I reckoned that soon enough I'd find out what it was like to put boots on the ground with him.

"You might have something there, Dunn," pondered Miller. "I recall oil was found a couple of years back south of here in Corsicana. Some bigwigs sniffed around, but there's not been any big oil find. It's certainly not enough to interest the Irish Mob, unless they know something we don't."

"I think they are anticipating a big find and looking to be fully set up to take advantage. That's why they were meddling with the railroads. Transporting oil will be important." I was thinking aloud, and Miller was listening intently.

"Wish we had a fly on the mule's rump," Miller speculated.

"You mean a person inside their operation?" I ventured. I felt a tad uncomfortable, as Miller laid contemplative eyes on me.

"It would have to be someone who knows what's going on," postulated the marshal.

I reckoned to get out ahead of Miller's thinking on this. There was no way I could go undercover. "Murphy and at least one of his henchmen know me," I said in an attempt to head off any suggestion that I go inside the Irish Mob.

"You own a fair-sized ranch down near Corpus Christi, don't you, Ranger Dunn?"

I nodded.

"How'd you like to get into the railroad business, but with aspirations of making a fortune in that black gold you mentioned?"

While the idea was intriguing, I was still concerned that Murphy would make me in a heartbeat. Plus, McClintock was still out to get me. "Where are you going with this, Marshal?"

"Did I hear that you resigned from the Texas Rangers to hook up with Uriah Lott in the railroad business?" asked Miller with a mischievous grin. "Yep, we could doll you up fancy like. Bankroll you to pursue railroads and oil."

I laughed nervously. "Railroads? Oil?" I gave the Deputy US Marshal a penetrating look.

"Oh, I'm dead serious, Ranger Dunn. We just have to make your good fortune so believable that the Irish Mob will overlook your past run-in with them. Greed has a way of overcoming good sense." Miller folded his hands on his desk. He seemed quite pleased with himself.

I had to admit to myself that the idea just might work. It certainly was worth considering.

Miller stood. "Sleep on it, Dunn. We'll talk further tomorrow morning." I saw in his eyes that so far as he was concerned, the matter was settled, and he was just giving me time to think about backing out. Now, I better understood the warning Captain Hughes gave me about Miller. By my bold actions, the marshal couldn't lose. He would risk nothing, while my life would be on the line.

It was a tad abrupt, but the meeting was over. I had to admit that the marshal had given me plenty to think about. First thing to do would be to let Cassie in on the plan and the risks, then contact Captain Hughes.

To be perfectly honest, I had far too much invested in wanting to bring down the Irish Mob. I knew from the moment I'd left Miller's office. Yep, Lucas Dunn Junior was going to uncork a brazen scheme to keep the Irish Mob out of Texas.

I telephoned Cassie. She had already endured three years of my service with the Texas Rangers and held fast to my promise of giving up the badge upon completion of the Irish Mob case. My cousins were true to their commitments to help out at the ranch, and Billy Skuggs was working out as foreman. I know she appreciated my letting her know about what I'd be doing. I'm not sure she fully appreciated all it would entail.

"I'm going to have to make a big deal out of separating from the Texas Rangers," I told her.

"What's that mean?" she asked.

"Some folks might not cotton to things I'll be saying. I have to make it believable. You might not be so popular with Corpus Christi society."

There was a momentary silence. Then, "I don't much care what they think."

"I'll be home in a couple of days to get things rolling," I said with a bit of relief at her acceptance of what could best be described as collateral social damage from the ruse I was about to initiate. "Bye, sweetie. I love you."

My next call was with Captain Hughes. I caught him just after dinner, so he was feeling right good. I explained that I'd met with Deputy US Marshal Miller, and it had gone well. "Miller came up with the idea that I should lure the Irish Mob into a trap. Since Murphy and his minions knew me, it wouldn't work to go undercover, per se. I needed to do something brassy; bold, if you will. I must have a major falling out with you. It must be believable."

"What's that supposed to lead to?" asked Hughes.

"Well, I'll start talking up my interests in railroads and exploring for oil. The marshal figured that it wouldn't take long for Murphy's folks to reach out to me. Greed seems to attract greed." I let that sink in. "I'm going to talk with Uriah Lott about building a railroad. I'll likely bring Archie Parr and the Railroad Commission of Texas into the mix to establish the seriousness of my intentions."

"Sounds as though you've made your decision," said Hughes. "Damned if it ain't bold as all Hell."

I laughed. "Guess that's about the size of it. I'll have to say some nasty things about you and the Rangers."

"Do what you have to do. Let me know if you need anything. When this works out, we'll throw down a couple of beers and figure what comes next." His use of the word *when* wasn't lost on me.

I hadn't the heart to tell Hughes about my promise to Cassie. We ended the call, and I headed to the hotel to sleep on all that was to happen. I recalled Deputy US Marshal Bass Reeves telling me about hiding in plain sight to catch a lawbreaker. It seemed that was now my game.

With my decision made, I reckoned to enjoy a fine steak at the Union Depot Hotel. The restaurant was crowded, but I was able to find a table. It was an establishment attempting to be refined, as white linen tablecloths and silver cutlery contrasted with mahogany-paneled walls and fine oak tables and chairs.

I ordered up a steak—rare, of course—with sides of corn

and potatoes. I passed on coffee, as I wanted a good night's sleep. Instead, I ordered a glass of wine.

A sweet-looking young lady soon placed my dinner before me. As I put my knife to a first morsel of steak, my eyes caught a figure of interest entering the establishment. None other than Gordon Murphy took a seat a few tables from me. He appeared to have aged a bit in the few months since I'd last seen him, as gray hair now appeared at his temples. His hand bore the scar from our previous encounter. His nose was a bit off kilter as though he'd been in a fight. I wondered that perhaps his bosses hadn't taken his failure in Dallas so well.

He had company. A dour-faced, slack-jawed man of wiry build joined him. The man's dark eyes coupled with a nasty scar down his left cheek gave him a decidedly evil appearance that his well-tailored burgundy velvet jacket failed to compensate for. He repeatedly dabbed at his hooked nose with a lace-trimmed handkerchief. The two looked to be the Devil's own.

I'm a tough man to miss in a crowd, given my size, so it was no surprise that Murphy's room-scanning eyes rested for just a moment upon me. He looked away furtively. It didn't take a mental giant to figure out that he was recalling my threat to him were he ever to return to Texas.

Rather than challenge Murphy in any way, I calmly finished my dinner. I reckoned to let him sweat a bit. When I'd finished, I paid the bill on my room tab and simply strode past him and his companion with nary a glance on my way out. I wanted to assure him, without the slightest direct engagement, that I was around and hadn't forgotten. I think he may have choked on his food as I passed.

I found myself actually relishing what I was about to undertake.

Miller's clerk knocked on the Deputy US Marshal's office door and announced my arrival.

"About time. Send him in," called out Miller. It sounded as though the marshal was anxious to get started.

I strode confidently into his office and took a seat. I glanced at the coffee pot on the credenza and laughed. "Still brewing that rotgut," I teased.

"Actually, I got here early and made some myself. It's from beans I had shipped up special from Galveston. Help yourself," he invited with a broad grin.

I busied myself pouring coffee while Miller opened our meeting topic.

"Appears to me that you've decided to agree with my plan to fool the Irish Mob right out of Texas," said Miller.

"You'd be right, Marshal. We just need to work a couple of things out."

Miller nodded in anticipation.

"First, I'll need a trusted point of contact with your office. Second, I'll need your influence to get a story into the local press about my bitter falling out with the Texas Rangers over my conflicting interest in railroads and oil."

"That's all?" queried Miller.

"I may come up with more, but that's all for now," I assured him, rubbing my chin thoughtfully.

"It'll be a pleasure working with you, Dunn." Miller paused, then lowered his voice to a near whisper. "My clerk is bought and paid for by certain folks to keep an eye on my office. Whatever he hears will be broadcast to those who pay him and likely a few more."

I nodded my understanding of the situation. "Oh, there is one more thing," I whispered concernedly. "Gordon Murphy employs a hired gun named Kyle McClintock. The man has a personal grudge against me that rises above what Murphy might assign to him."

"What about this McClintock fella?" pressed Miller.

"He's wanted for a variety of crimes, including attempted murder and attempted rape." I tried to keep the personal passion out of my voice.

"And, he's tried to kill you," added Miller.

I nodded.

"We'll bring him in. Anything else?" Miller pulled out a scratch pad and wrote himself a reminder to bring McClintock in.

"The coffee was much improved, Marshal Miller," I said good-humoredly, loudly enough for the clerk to hear.

The marshal stood and extended his hand.

We shook.

"Are you ready?" I teased.

"Go for it," responded Miller.

I slammed my fist on Miller's desk loud enough for his clerk to hear. "I'll not stand for that sort of crap, Marshal!" I hollered. "I'll be damned if you're putting me up to it."

"Calm down," said Miller loudly.

"Calm, hell! In fact, to hell with the Texas Rangers!" I stalked out of Miller's office, slamming the door nearly hard enough to shatter the glass.

The clerk sat aghast as I strode defiantly past and out the door. I smiled to myself, as I headed for the Union Depot Hotel to grab my bag.

Soon enough, I was on the train headed back to Corpus Christi.

SIX
PARTING OF THE WAYS

FROM CORPUS CHRISTI, I sent a ciphered telegram for Captain Hughes to meet me as soon as possible. It was an unusual request, so I reckoned he'd respond right quickly. Importantly, we'd have to meet secretly. To frustrate anyone attempting to break the code, my message told him there was a problem with the ferry at Nuecestown. I figured it was a bizarre enough ploy to fend off curious interceptors and even intrigue the captain. I was grateful that we'd discussed encrypted messaging before my taking on this assignment. Cipher techniques had been used decades earlier during the War Between the States, so we weren't reinventing the practice.

As I rode up the lane to our ranch house, I thought on the bittersweet situation before me. I was responsible for a thriving ranch, yet had to fulfill my Texas Ranger obligation. I was to become a thespian of sorts, acting out a role for which I was fully unequipped. Like my dad, I'd been raised to be humble, whether under the mantel of success or failure. How I'd be acting was like oil and water in my psyche. Once begun, I dared not back away until the job was completed. All the while, I still had to deal with the lingering threat of Kyle McClintock.

Cassie was overjoyed to have me back at Heaven's Gate.

I quickly explained my plan to infiltrate the Irish Mob. She took it stoically.

"It won't be easy," I concluded. "The community will give you a rough time thinking I'm at odds with the Texas Rangers. They are going to see a seemingly bigger-than-life, full-of-himself rancher. They won't and can't know what I'm up to. We dare not even tell our folks. My boastings of oil riches will find their way to Dallas, and then the plan kicks in earnestly. I'll be dancing the two-step with that nest of rattlesnakes."

Cassie broke into an irony-laden grin. "There are gossips I'd just as soon not have anything to do with, Lucas. Guess we'll see who our true friends are." She was about to pour coffee, but paused. "What about your Texas Ranger cousins?"

"Hrumph!" I guffawed. "I'll bet they'll be on to my game in no time. They'll be savvy enough to not give it away."

"A wink and a nod?" postulated Cassie.

"Yep," I responded with confidence. I took a long sip of coffee. "I've got to meet Captain Hughes in the morning. It shouldn't take long. It's important that he be fully onboard and act his part. He'll be called to say a couple of nasty things about me to convince the mob of my cutting ties with the Rangers."

Little did I know that Gordon Murphy and his evil-looking sidekick were more than a little concerned about me. I'd become an obsessively regular topic of conversation after the breakfast encounter back in Dallas. I reckoned their conversation went something like:

"Just get rid of him," urged the man who apparently served as Murphy's aide.

"Tried that. It's not so easy. The man has eyes in the back of his head," responded Murphy.

"Come now. How many men have we hired for just this sort of assignment?" The man absentmindedly traced his finger along the dark scar that ran up his cheek. Any observer might expect his tongue to dart out like a serpent.

"There's rumor that he left the Texas Rangers. He inherited a big ranch and wants to explore for oil."

"I don't trust him. Nobody turns that quickly."

I'd have loved to have been a fly on the wall for just such a conversation. In any case, I heard that Marshal Miller was doing a good job of spreading the big rumor about me to the right folks to blabber around town. Having done a little homework, I learned that the Irish Mob was a collection of what folks called organized crime syndicates. The families were primarily composed of ethnic Irish members, operating primarily in Ireland, the United States, the United Kingdom, Canada, and Australia.

In New York, they originated from Irish-American street gangs. They ruled through violence, taking protection money while inflicting the likes of assault, murder, bribery, fraud, illegal gambling, prostitution, and more. With the Dallas operations, they hoped to tap into the potential lurking with oil. Folks were calling it black gold, and that had been enough to attract the Irish Mob.

I'd ridden in on Upriver Road along the south shore of the Nueces River. For a while, I stood in shadows among the pecan trees within a few yards of the ferry that had plied the river for decades. I recalled my dad telling me how Colonel Kinney had built the ferry to facilitate travel to Corpus Christi. Nuecestown had sprung up around it. As the river flowed past, I debated myself. Was my decision to meet Captain Hughes face-to-face wise or foolish? I sort of hoped in any case someone would overhear our conversation, and it would get back to Gordon Murphy.

I finally sucked it in and headed for the old Stagecoach Inn. It was a decrepit shadow of its former self, as stagecoaches had been replaced by the iron horse. I hitched Tornado.

I scanned the room as I entered. About half of the dozen tables were occupied. There were a couple of folks who looked familiar, but I couldn't say that I actually knew them. There was an oppressive dustiness in the air, laden with the aroma of bacon grease. I spied Hughes and ambled over. "Morning, Captain," I growled by way of greeting.

Hughes looked off across the room as though he was ignoring me. "Who the hell you think you are?" He said this loudly enough that anyone overhearing would be convinced that the captain was none too pleased with me. "You going to infiltrate the Irish Mob?" he said with a barely audible murmur.

I roughly grabbed the chair opposite him but didn't sit. I loomed over Hughes as he sipped his coffee. "You heard right, dammit! I quit!" I retorted. "Yes. You support this?" I whispered.

Hughes offered a barely perceptible nod. "Well, don't look for any thanks from me, you sonofabitch! You're a damned quitter!" he boomed. His face had reddened enough to convince anyone watching that he was angry with me.

"I need the name of Murphy's number two," I whispered, then, "Well, damn you and the Rangers anyway. I've got bigger fish to fry! I'm going to find oil and be rich!" I was almost a little too loud.

"I'll find out." I could barely hear Hughes' response. The Texas Ranger captain stood and leaned toward me with his hand on the butt of his Colt and a finger wagging in my face. "Have it your way, Dunn. Get your sorry ass out of my sight!" he exclaimed.

I clenched my fists. "Damn you!" I said by way of goodbye. I stalked away, mounted up, and rode off.

The patrons in the inn were surely left aghast at what they'd witnessed. Word would travel the gossip mill faster than greased lightning.

I rode under the lavender early morning sky for about two miles, when I heard the galloping hooves of a horse approach from behind me. I reined in and strained my eyes to identify the rider. Coming from the east with the sun behind him, he was effectively a hazy silhouette. As he drew near, the rider's image became increasingly familiar. Kyle McClintock! I instinctively went for my Smith & Wesson.

"No need! Hold your fire!" shouted McClintock with both hands raised. He pulled up roughly ten feet from me.

"What do you want, you mangy sonofabitch?" I challenged.

"Mr. Murphy asked me to check up on you. He wanted to know whether you've really had a falling out with the Texas Rangers."

"And?" I felt rage coming on deep within me. I wanted to bust McClintock's chops to within an inch of his life.

"I overheard your chat with your boss. I guess I should say former boss."

"You got that right. And you can tell your boss that I'm hunting for black gold. Maybe I'll find it first."

McClintock smiled. "Let's let bygones be bygones, Junior."

"That's Luke Dunn to you, McClintock," I snarled. "My dad passed. I'm not using the *junior* anymore." I gave him the most steely-eyed look I could muster. "We'll see about bygones. I haven't forgotten what you did to Cassie, and neither did she. I ought to kill you right here and now." I waved the muzzle of my Smith & Wesson toward him.

McClintock's crooked smile oozed overconfidence. "Well, that'd be murder, wouldn't it, Mr. *former* Texas Ranger?" He emphasized *former*. With that, he laughed, wheeled his horse, and galloped off.

I sat my saddle while my insides burned with anger born of frustration. "Just wait," I whispered to myself through clenched teeth. My day would yet come. And Gordon Murphy? He had a lot of *cajones* sending McClintock to spy on me.

SEVEN
THE PLOT THICKENS

AS I RODE up the lane from the gateway arch, I was still seething from my encounter with McClintock. The lowlife knew I wouldn't kill him, though I wished he'd drawn close enough that I could have beaten him to within an inch of his worthless life.

I rode straight to the barn. A few minutes currying Tornado might serve to calm me enough to face Cassie and my boys. Brody and Tess greeted me at the barn door with tails wagging. Dogs could have a soothing effect on the human psyche, and these two were quite effective at it. Between my Appaloosa stallion and the two dogs, I was soon in my right mind. I finished up and headed for the house.

Bode and Sean met me about halfway, and a smiling Cassie waved to me from the gallery. This was home, and I loved it.

"How did your meeting go?" asked Cassie, as I mounted the steps with a laughing son in each arm and dogs nipping at my heels.

"Short and effective," I replied. "By tomorrow, word will be all over Texas."

"What's next?" she asked.

I was almost embarrassed to say. "Well, I'm going to have to upgrade my wardrobe a tad. I need to look like someone of means. I'll have to go to Corpus and buy some new clothes."

Cassie smiled. "Well, I'm up for that. I could use a few things myself."

I reckoned it made sense to take the family. I needed to give off the impression that I was done with the Texas Rangers. Taking the family shopping in the city would be a great way to feed the image of separation from law enforcement that I was trying to project.

Cassie sidled up to me. "I think I might come to like this assignment."

I looked down into her eyes. "Don't be lulling yourself into a false sense of security. There's sure to be danger ahead. Meanwhile, I must build my image as an oil entrepreneur and patiently wait for the Irish Mob to approach me. Then comes the tough part…getting them to trust me enough to infiltrate their organization. Once I get enough evidence, I'll turn it over to the Deputy US Marshal. The mob will be spitting mad."

Cassie hugged me. "If anyone can do this, it's you, Lucas."

I appreciated her confidence.

Our journey to Corpus Christi was quite an affair. Bode and Sean were bundled into the back seat, though we drew a line at bringing the dogs. I tied Tornado to the rear of the carriage just in case there was trouble.

We pulled up late morning at the Cacti & Boots haberdashery. Our old friends Scarlett and Carson Walker ran the place, so we felt confident that they'd take good care of us. I stepped down and helped Cassie from the seat. While she tended to the boys, I headed up to the wooden sidewalk across the front of the store. As I stood there awaiting Cassie, I heard the lock turn in the door behind me and turned to see a window shade being pulled down. A *closed* sign appeared.

Cassie had just joined me and spotted the sign. "Well, that's a fine howdy-do from friends," she observed.

I sighed. "Guess the word's gotten out."

"Well, I'm not putting up with this sort of thing!" exclaimed Cassie. She took a step toward the door.

I grabbed her arm. "We can't tell them the truth, Cassie." I shook my head resignedly. "Maybe we can find a shop elsewhere in Corpus." I sincerely doubted it, but reckoned to give it a try.

After a couple of hours of meeting with stores closed to us, we decided to head home.

"Let's head to Alice tomorrow," suggested Cassie, as we headed back to Heaven's Gate.

"It's still too close, sweetheart. We'll have to make do with what we have for now. Maybe my dad left some fashionable duds that'll fit me. I'm not sure about you."

"I'll get over it, Lucas. Hopefully, we can get back to a normal life sooner than later."

As it turned out, I did manage to find a couple of serviceable suits from my dad's wardrobe. My mom hadn't seen fit to dispose of his personals just yet. Now, I had to climb into my role as a scion of ranching and oil.

Oil? Where might oil be found in Texas? I knew that the first producing oil well had been drilled up at Oil Springs in Nacogdoches County back in 1866 and produced roughly ten barrels per day. Turned out that it wasn't enough to make it economically feasible. It wasn't until four years back that an oilfield in Corsicana was discovered while drilling for water. This led to what folks marked as the first Texas oil boom. Nearly 300 wells were producing oil in this field. Undoubtedly, this had to be drawing the attention of Gordon Murphy.

I wasn't going to be so financially foolhardy as to drill for oil on Heaven's Gate Ranch, but I reckoned to connect with the folks up in Corsicana as a first step. I also wondered when Murphy would reach out to me.

Cassie and I accommodated the attitudes of folks as best we could. There's no accounting for the perceptions people generate based on rumors and half-truths. I looked forward to the gushing apologies that would eventually come forth after I helped chase the Irish Mob from Texas. I was confident that I'd succeed…confident but not cocksure. Meanwhile, I had a part to play in this theater of the absurd. I also had a lot to learn about the particulars of the oil business, so I reckoned to head to Corsicana in the next day or two.

I received an encrypted message from Captain Hughes to the effect that Murphy's number two was a man with a long list of arrests back in New York City. His name was Colin O'Neal. It weighed on me as to the contrast of my Irish-ancestry cousins here in Texas, who labored peacefully to make a living and raise families, and the violent versions of my Irish heritage that made parts of New York City a living hell and sought to bring that evil to Texas. They'd not run into the likes of me enough and would wish they hadn't.

Did I look like a man intent on investing in oil? I wore a gray vested wool suit with black boots. My pants were held up by this new-fangled fashion called a belt. A watch was stuffed in my vest pocket with its gold chain dangling from the bezel. I wore a white shirt with a cravat and topped off my costume with a Stetson featuring a cattleman's crease in its crown. I carried a black leather satchel containing my traveling effects and a change of clothes. Oh, and I did have my Smith & Wesson tucked into a holster under my arm.

As I sat my seat on the train headed north, I had the sense that I was being spied upon. It was not unlike the feeling I'd had when I worked on the case in Kerrville and went to visit Bass Reeves up at Fort Smith. Back then, I had that shiny Texas Ranger badge pinned to my chest. Now, I was a civilian. In that case, a ne'er-do-well named Garth Jones had tailed me. I sat there trying not to be obvious in scanning the passengers in the car. Who might be tailing me? It sure wasn't Kyle McClintock. No one looked the least bit suspicious, yet I knew it had to be one of these folks. Was I paranoid? Be that as it may, I reckoned they wouldn't dare do anything violent.

The clicking of steel over rail joints soon lulled me to sleep. Even the horn announcing railroad crossings and squeal of brakes at depots failed to awaken me. Mile after mile flew by. The conductor awakened me once, so I could transfer to a train headed for Corsicana. It didn't take me long to return to peaceful somnolence.

I thought on the message from Captain Hughes identifying Murphy's enforcer as Colin O'Neal. The man bore a quaint-enough Irish name as cover for a life quite clearly committed to violence. I'd heard such a vile creature referred to as an enforcer, a man whose role was to ensure that the dictates of his mob employers were met. I rather looked forward to meeting the man. The question of when and how lingered along with under what circumstances. In any case, I likely had to pass muster with O'Neal to gain the confidence of Murphy. Hopefully, word had spread of my poisonous parting with Marshal Miller and with the Texas Rangers.

EIGHT
GETTING MY FEET WET

I CAN'T SAY that Corsicana exceeded my expectations. My first task was to make myself known as a man interested in oil ventures. It obviously entailed more than simply running a newspaper ad promoting my interests. I had to be low-key. Braggadocio was too over the top to put on. I had money, but dared not flash it around. Nope, I needed to make solid acquaintances.

The oil boom town had a population of more than six thousand folks, most of them connected to the oil business. My search for connections had to be whittled down. While I could have strode into most any saloon, the clientele was unlikely to be frequented by the folks I sought. I reckoned my best bet was to meet the mayor. Could I simply walk in on the mayor? Why not? If I wanted to become a Texas oil magnate big enough to draw the interest of Gordon Murphy, I had to be rather forthright about my intentions.

I checked into the Molloy Hotel, a two-story structure built better than two decades ago. The hotel had a reputation as a center for business and social activities, so it made great sense to secure lodging there. The clerk was a helpful fellow.

I signed my name in the register with a flourish. "My name is Lucas Dunn. I've sold some ranching interests in South Texas and looking to get into the oil business in a serious way. I hear tell that Corsicana is the place to do just that. Where might a businessman such as myself engage around these parts with like-minded folks?"

The clerk offered a respectful smile. "Why, Mr. Dunn, our dining room hosts many of the folks you seek." He handed me my room key. "I suggest dinner around seven, sir."

"And where might I find the mayor of this fine town, young man? I believe his name is Woods."

"Oh, yes, sir. Mayor Woods office is in city hall, not far from the train depot," he said, then smiled. "He often dines here of an evening."

"Much obliged. I appreciate your help," I replied and left a quarter on the open register. I picked up my bag and was about to turn away but paused. "How might I gain an introduction to Mayor Woods?"

The clerk's smile broadened. "You need no introduction, Mr. Dunn. He likely already knows you're in town." His smile turned to one of the more mischievous variety. "The mayor eats quite well, if you catch my drift, Mr. Dunn. He's hard to miss."

As recommended, I showed up at the hotel dining room just a tad before seven in the evening. A bath, shave, and fresh shirt cleared away any travel dust and made me presentable as seeking to be a rising star in the oil industry. A lovely young lady escorted me to a table. "Pardon, but might Mayor Woods be here?" I'd already scanned the room and seen no one answering the hotel clerk's description.

"No, sir, but I'll be pleased to inform you when he arrives," she replied.

"Thank you." It was reassuring to know that Woods was expected.

I ordered a steak dinner appropriate to a man of my station, along with a glass of wine. My venture into the oil business was not going to be cheap for Texas.

Mayor James Hollins Woods turned out to be a portly fellow, as intimated by the hotel clerk. Muttonchop sideburns framed his face, and he projected the engaging, charismatic personality of a politician. There was no question that he was connected and likely holding higher political ambitions.

As I was about to carve into the savory steak set before me, who walks in but Mayor Woods. He was every bit as portly as I'd been led to expect. He was friendly with the patrons, even giving me a smile as though he'd known me for years. The server seated him at what must have been his regular table. It offered a vantage point by which all restaurant patrons could be seen and, importantly, could see him.

Just a couple of minutes after Woods was seated, a lanky gentleman strode in and seated himself opposite Woods. It appeared that the two had business to discuss.

I didn't want to appear overly anxious and was not about to miss enjoying my dinner. Woods would have to wait a bit. I did keep an eye on him, chuckling to myself when a rather large steak with two baked potatoes was placed before him. He was not seeking to lose weight.

I finished my dinner then sat back and sipped coffee, as I sized up Woods and his companion. Finally, I pulled myself together and sauntered over to Woods' table.

"Pardon, Mr. Woods. My name is…"

"Why, Mr. Dunn! I've been told you'd be looking for me." He offered a smile and his hand.

"Yes, sir," I said, shaking his hand.

"Do have a seat. This is Karl Aimes. He manages my financial interests," offered Woods.

I shook Aimes' hand and took a seat. I had learned that Woods dabbled in real estate loans and even owned a bookstore, so his financial dealing likely required an accountant such as Aimes. "Pleasure to meet y'all. Since you know my name, I expect you know why I'm here in Corsicana."

Woods laughed and took a sip of his wine. He drew a cigar from his coat breast pocket, then a second, which he offered to me.

"Thanks, but no. My horse hates its smell on my breath." I strove for a little humor.

Woods laughed a tad more heartily. "Heard you were a rancher. Guess you have to keep your cayuse happy." He cast a look at Aimes. "I understand that you had a falling out with the Texas Rangers. Guess the Rangers run a tight outfit."

I didn't want to get into a spitting discussion about the Texas Rangers, so shifted the subject. "I'm interested in oil, Mr. Woods."

"Well, you've come to the right place for that," he responded with a wink to Aimes.

"I'd like to invest, but need the right connection," I ventured. "You wouldn't happen to know a financier out of Dallas named Gordon Murphy?

Woods was unruffled, as he took another sip of wine. Aimes looked uncomfortable.

"Do you know of him, Karl?" he asked.

"Just rumors, sir. Some say he's with some Irish gang out of New York City," responded Aimes.

"You may rest assured that we stay clear of that sort, Mr. Dunn," said Woods with a seemingly jaundiced eye to Aimes. "Why do you ask?"

I reckoned that Woods recognized that it wouldn't do for a man with political aspirations to be tied to something as nefarious as the Irish Mob. "Just curious. I'd heard rumors, too. I understand that they are interested in the oil business."

"Well, they won't be welcome in Corsicana, Mr. Dunn. You can take that to the bank," Woods said with a firm set to his jaw. He dabbed with a napkin at a bit of sweat alongside one of his sideburns.

"That's reassuring. I sure wouldn't want to be mixed up with those sorts of fellows." The server placed a cup of coffee before me. "Now, as to who to do business with around here? And I'd like to learn more about how the business side works."

"Good that you recognize your shortcomings, Mr. Dunn. You don't want to make foolhardy investments." Woods leaned back and folded his hands over his belly. "I suggest you look up Waylon Weatherby. He'll tell you all you need to know about the business side."

"I appreciate that, Mr. Woods. I'll look him up. I do need to figure where to best invest my money." I figured that I'd learn more from Woods at a later time. With Aimes there, I didn't want to arouse any suspicions as to my intentions. Something about Aimes didn't feel right. Woods seemed to be a straight shooter. I stood. "Thanks kindly for your advice, Mr. Woods. I reckon to stay here for a couple of days and expect I'll see you around town." With that, I left the dining room.

I did need to make an investment, if for no other reason than to get the word back to Murphy that I was a serious player in the oil business. It wasn't too late, so I figured to grab a drink before turning in.

I headed to the Iron Front Saloon on Beaton Street. The place was bustling fairly well for a Thursday evening, though I imagined that it reached its heights of action on the weekend. Oil drilling was a round-the-clock activity, so laborers would visit at all hours.

As I sidled up to the bar, I wasn't surprised to see a few roughnecks laughing over beer around a table in a rear corner while drillers and managers commiserated separately. A couple of scantily dressed ladies kept drinks flowing. I say they were dressed provocatively, but it didn't appear that any sort of illicit endeavors were going on. I ordered a whiskey and ambled over to the only empty table to sit and relax a bit.

I took in the various goings on around the barroom. It was rather fascinating to watch the styles of interactions among the patrons. Behaviors appeared to be dependent upon how their jobs reflected their stations in life.

In my peripheral vision, I noticed the barkeep whispering in the ear of a particularly attractive barmaid. Her dress left little to the imagination, especially as her breasts barely stayed within the bounds of her bodice. I didn't think much of it, even as she eased on over near my table.

It took just a few seconds. She was suddenly in my lap, posing provocatively, and planting a kiss on my cheek as a photographer snapped a picture of us.

"Thank you," she cooed as she left as quickly as she'd come. Of course, the photographer was nowhere to be seen. It caused nary a ripple of attention around the room.

Call it paranoia, but I sensed that Murphy was behind

this stunt. I reckoned the photograph was going to cost me. I shrugged, finished my drink, and headed back to the hotel.

There was nothing I could do about the incident at the Iron Front Saloon, so there was no point in fretting over it. Shucks, I didn't even know the young lady's name. Only time would tell as to when or where the intended blackmail might come into play. I didn't figure to lose any sleep over it, as I'd encountered worse situations concerning wanton women in my Texas Ranger career. Besides, Cassie knew that I was true blue. Meanwhile, I decided to take Woods' advice and look up Mr. Weatherby.

NINE

OIL MAGNATE!

"HOWDY, Mr. Weatherby. I'm Luke Dunn. Jim Woods suggested I meet you," I said in a loud voice intended to overcome the noise of the oil drilling rig. I reckoned it was a comfortable enough introduction attempt, as I walked up to Weatherby at one of the clusters of three rigs.

Weatherby looked curiously at me. "I ain't deaf, son."

I extended my hand.

"Woods sent you, eh?" He shook my hand and managed a weak smile. "It's a tad busy around here right now. Go wait over at yonder line shack, and I'll be with you in about thirty minutes."

I nodded and found my way over to the shack he'd pointed out. I took a seat on a bench out front, where I had a birds-eye view of the drilling operations. The contrast between Weatherby in his gray wool suit and derby hat was stark, as distinguished from the sweaty, grimy roughnecks and drillers working the rig. Yet, I had the impression that at some point, Weatherby had worked the rigs just as the roughnecks did. Watching the precision of the drilling was a sight to behold. It was dangerous and required teamwork to avoid injuries.

As I'd already learned, there were four essential elements to the oil drilling process. The drill bit cut through rock and earth to create the wellbore while the drill pipe transmitted the rotary motion and carried drilling mud. The derrick supported the rotating drill bit as it gouged into the earth. The fourth critical part was drilling mud, which was circulated to remove debris and cool the bit. Here in Corsicana, steam engines were engaged to a cogwheel-driven rotary system. It was a fascinating process that extracted this invaluable product nicknamed black gold. I understood that this rotary drilling method could reach depths of thirty thousand feet. I reckoned that I knew enough to get by.

It was a long thirty minutes of watching Weatherby cajole and coddle the oil rig crew as they sought to overcome some sort of problem deep under the surface. He finally headed my way.

"Sorry about the delay, son. Damned foreman didn't think he could drill any deeper, but I convinced him otherwise." Weatherby looked up at me as though trying to remember something. "You say your name's Dunn?"

I realized that we weren't speaking loudly anymore, as we were farther from the rig. Talking in a normal tone had a relaxing effect. "That's me. Mayor Woods suggested that you would be helpful toward my investing in this booming industry."

Weatherby laughed. "Let's hope the boom holds. Seems to be plenty of oil so far as we can tell. Likely change the Texas economy a bit."

It was clear that Weatherby understated the impact on Texas. Cattle and cotton had shaped the state's economy for decades, and oil would enhance the state's bounty for many years to come. "I'm of a mind to shape my own drilling company."

Weatherby shook his head. "You'd better have plenty of money, son. It's a tough business to break into, and there are some unsavory folks already salivating like wolves to carve out choice pieces. I've even heard that the Railroad Commission is looking to dabble in oil."

"I have plenty of resources, Mr. Weatherby. I'm looking for advice on who would be best to do business with."

"There's really only one company right now. It's run by Joe Cullinan. Shoot, he was drilling for water when the first Corsicana well came in. Other than Joe's operation, the only other outfit that might be interested would be the Gladys City Oil, Gas, and Manufacturing Company. Some fellow named Tony Lucas is helping them out. Were I a betting man, I'd lay my money on Cullinan." Weatherby rubbed his chin distractedly, as though having lapsed into deep thought. "How'd you like to spend a few days on a rig?"

I smiled and shook my head. "I've mucked stables, handled hay bales, and stepped in plenty of cowpies, Mr. Weatherby. I'm not ready to get so deep into the oil business as you suggest."

"Guess you'll be keeping that nice suit you're wearing right clean then," responded Weatherby. "There's nothing like wrestling an oil bit to throw fear of the wrath of God into you. If you decide to get dirty, let me know."

"Thanks kindly. I do reckon to meet a few folks yet today, but I'll keep your offer in mind." I knew in the very depths of my soul that hugging a drill bit wasn't in my plans.

It wasn't difficult to see that becoming an oil magnate was not going to be an overnight endeavor. I needed a breakout moment of sorts. I figured this Cullinan fellow mentioned by Weatherby was pretty much settled into his oil business. What reason would he have to deal with an upstart like me?

I needed to find others looking to break into the game. It wouldn't hurt if they were just a tad dirty, as that might be attractive to Murphy. This thinking led me to wonder what Murphy—for surely it was Murphy—had in mind with the compromising photograph from the Iron Front Saloon. While Corsicana was where the drilling action was, it seemed to me that Dallas or Houston would be more likely to domicile folks interested in investing in black gold. Dallas made the most sense, given that it was where the Irish Mob had decided to take root.

Corsicana was a nice enough town, but I boarded a train next morning bound for Dallas. I intended to bring Gordon Murphy out into the open by blatantly flaunting my investment intentions. I reckoned to spin my interest by letting it be known that I intended to control to a level that challenged the Irish Mob's aspirations.

I sat back and tried to relax so far as relaxation was possible on the wooden slat seats in the aged coach I'd boarded. It was a smaller railroad car with fewer travelers. I attributed the sparse ridership to the discomfort, as modern cars featured padded bench seats. It did give me a splendid view of the passengers. I still had the feeling I was being shadowed but remained unable to identify the culprit that was tailing me. There were a couple of shady-looking characters, but there was no hard and fast rule that spies had to wear a special uniform of the trade. I kept my Smith & Wesson handy, not that I expected any trouble just yet.

The question of where to go in Dallas rolled over in my mind. I considered that a banker might be a good start, if I could find one willing to be chatty. Moving my money into a local bank seemed a reasonable ploy to get acquainted.

TEN
BUSINESS GUSHER

THE TRAIN RIDE from Corsicana was uneventful save for that danged uncomfortable seat. Upon arrival in Dallas around midday, I stepped gingerly to the platform and paused to see who else disembarked. It was perhaps a disappointment that at least a dozen passengers left the train. If one of them was following me, he or she was doing a good job of being indistinguishable from the crowd. It was nothing like when Garth Jones was following me, as he made himself rather obvious.

I shrugged and headed for the Union Depot Hotel.

"Y'all have a room for a tired traveler?" I asked the clerk.

The clerk looked me up and down before deciding whether I was worthy of his attention. This was a different front desk clerk from the one I'd previously dealt with. "How long might you be staying with us, Mr. ...?"

"Dunn...Lucas Dunn. I expect I just might be here a week or so."

"Have you stayed with us before?" the clerk inquired.

"Yes." His use of *us* sounded welcoming but overly contrived.

"Well, Mr. Dunn, I believe we do have accommodations available. Of course, we ask for payment in advance."

For some strange reason, I guess I felt edgy enough to want to shove *us* and *we* down the young man's throat. "That's no problem, young man."

"If you'd be so kind as to sign our guest register." He thrust the ledger toward me with a room key.

I signed and took the key. As he was about to take the register back, I stopped him with my hand firmly on the register. "Where might I find the most reputable bank in Dallas?"

The clerk looked at me as though I was asking for the best bank to rob. He yanked at the register, but I held firm.

"I wish to make a deposit. I'm investing in the oil business and need a good local bank." As I spoke, I mentally calculated how long it would take for news of my arrival and oil interest to spread around Dallas thanks to this young man behind the hotel register.

"Well, Mr. Dunn, I understand that the First National Bank of Dallas has a fine reputation." He delivered his advice with his chest proudly puffed out as though a veritable font of invaluable information. "First National is very well established."

"I see." I rubbed my chin, feigning thoughtfulness. "Any other bank you might recommend?" I asked with a wink.

The clerk leaned over the counter and cupped his hand to his mouth. "There's the Dallas Trust, Mr. Dunn," he said in a near whisper.

I released the ledger. "Is that some sort of secret?" I asked in an equally low voice.

The clerk looked about. "Boss likes to promote First National when patrons ask."

"Well, I appreciate your help." I laid a quarter on the counter. "I'd appreciate a bath at your earliest convenience." With that, I turned, picked up my satchel, and headed for my room.

With a bath, shave, and fresh shirt, I felt like a new man. I reckoned that I looked the part of a respectable oil man. As I stepped from the hotel, I'd already decided to make the venerable Dallas Trust my first stop in this fine city.

I passed the building that housed Gordon Murphy and had the creepy feeling that he or one of his people was watching me. They very well could have been. By now, he had to know that I was in town and even that I was planning on doing a bit of banking.

Before leaving the Union Depot Hotel, I did learn that the president of the Dallas Trust was a fellow named Ernest Carson.

The Dallas Trust building looked like a bank. That was the best way to describe it. It was built of stone with four columns out front and three granite steps leading to very secure-looking double doors made of oak with oversized iron door handles. I kicked the street dust from my boots and bounced on up to those doors. I took a deep breath and entered.

Would it be surprising to find myself greeted by Mr. Carson his very self? My but word traveled fast. I extended my hand. "Mr. Carson? I'm Luke Dunn."

"Yessir, Mr. Dunn. I was told you'd be visiting our fine establishment." He smiled as though mentally counting my net worth. He was dressed in a dark suit with a buttoned vest that threatened to burst open thanks to his rather prodigious midsection. He wore wire-rimmed glasses and had combed back what little hair remained on his head. I wondered whether the sprouts of hair from his ears compensated for what was missing on his head.

"Please join me in my office," he said and led the way past the vault and to his office at the rear of the bank. It was more modestly appointed than I'd expected. The desk and chairs were handsome but not ornate. There was a small secretarial desk with a few papers and a decanter on top and two chairs. The walls featured mahogany paneling, and bookcases contained a mix of business and entertainment reading. A large gilt-framed oil painting of the Alamo dominated the wall opposite Carson's desk. Behind the desk was a large window with a view of a well-landscaped park featuring bluebonnets.

I sat in the rather comfortable chair he motioned me to.

He took his seat behind the desk. There's something about doing business with a man behind a desk that I find less than desirable. It put the person behind the desk in control. "Care for a cigar, Mr. Dunn? Or perhaps some of our fine Dallas whiskey?"

I demurred. "Thanks, Mr. Carson, but I'll save any drinking for later, and I don't smoke."

"Nothing like clean living," he observed. He leaned forward and was about to inquire about my banking needs.

I stood and walked over to the bookcase. I picked a book randomly and sat at the small desk.

Carson seemed to catch my drift. It was obviously uncomfortable for him, but he arose and took the seat opposite me.

Once he was seated, I dropped the book on the table and gave him one of my steely, *I-mean-business* looks.

Carson swallowed hard. It must have been difficult for him to not be in control. "How may Dallas Trust help you?"

"I'm looking to invest a sizable sum in oil, Mr. Carson. I decided that a local banking establishment would be more convenient than back near my ranch south of San Antonio."

"You're a rancher?" asked Carson.

I nodded. "Just a modest hundred and fifty thousand acres or so. I sold some cattle and a bit of land with the intention of investing in the oil business. I was in Corsicana the past couple of days learning what I could about what some are calling black gold and reckoned that Dallas would become a hub for the industry."

"You're right on that account, Mr. Dunn." He rubbed his chubby little hands together.

"I'm looking to transfer a hundred thousand dollars from my bank in Corpus Christi. I was assured that Dallas Trust could handle that sort of sum." I thought Carson was about to swallow his tongue at the mention of money.

He brought himself together and sat upright. "Why, I do believe we can handle such a sum, Mr. Dunn," he assured me.

I leaned toward the banker in a confidential manner. "I'm also looking for a couple of partners. I'm sure that someone as well connected with the community as you would be able to connect me with financially solid folks with interests similar to mine."

Carson's eyes grew large and might have turned the color of money. "Why, I'd be pleased to make some introductions, Mr. Dunn." He rubbed his hands reflexively. "There's a rather well-heeled group meeting tomorrow evening at the Union Depot Hotel. You might find among them the sort of partners you're seeking. The meeting is in a back room and requires a special invitation. I can see that you receive one."

"I'd be much obliged," I said with a satisfied smile. I wondered whether Murphy or O'Neal would be in attendance, though that would be rather bold of them. Surely, they'd have a surrogate. With that, I stood. "I assume you'll accept a draft against my account in Corpus?"

"Absolutely, Mr. Dunn. We can do that right here."

Within fifteen minutes, I found myself emerging from Dallas Trust into the afternoon of a beautiful sunny day. The faint aroma of the nearby Fort Worth stockyards danced across my nose. I rather missed Heaven's Gate Ranch and surely missed Cassie. I promised myself to give her a call from the hotel.

I enjoyed a phone call with Cassie and felt assured that all was well at the ranch. I told her about the little photograph incident at the Iron Front Saloon, and we had a good laugh. I didn't share with her that I feared the Irish Mob just might take advantage of my absence from Heaven's Gate to exact a bit of insurance against any dealings we might yet have. By now, word of my activities surely had to have reached Murphy's ears.

As I strolled toward the hotel, I sensed that I was being followed. It would be premature for anything untoward to happen, so I shrugged it off as part of this business I was now wrapped up in. I decided to turn up a random alley. The man I suspected of being my tail didn't follow.

I waited a few minutes.

"Mr. Dunn?"

I turned to see the man who had been following me. He had US Marshal written all over him.

"Just wanted to let you know that we're around and

have your backtrail." With that, he turned and walked away.

I stood there dumbfounded. "Stupid sonofabitch," I mumbled to myself. Why not paint a target on my back? Trying not to be too obvious, I looked around to see whether whoever was tailing me had seen the marshal. Far as I could make out, the coast was clear. When this case was over, I promised myself that I'd have a few choice words for Marshal Miller.

Still seething a bit, I made my way back to the Union Depot Hotel. I stalked past the desk clerk and made my way up the stairs to my room on the second floor. I figured to relax a bit before dinner. I opened the door to my room and found an envelope that had been slipped under the door. So much for relaxation.

I slit it open with my knife and pulled out a perfumed piece of paper and a photograph. Of course, the photo was of me and the pretty young lady at the Iron Front Saloon back in Corsicana. There was no note; just the photo. I actually found myself smiling.

It was likely that Gordon Murphy had been promptly made aware of the money transfer to the Dallas Trust. I had the banker pegged for a man easily bought.

I stuffed the photo into my vest pocket for safekeeping.

Having enjoyed a fine steak dinner the night before, I arose early to find another envelope slipped under my room door. This was getting to be a habit.

I slit open the envelope and pulled out a rather fancy-looking card. It turned out that Mr. Ernest Carson was good on his word to get me an invitation to the gathering in the back room of the hotel tonight. The affair was at seven o'clock and included a dinner.

The day was sunny, warm, and dry, so I poked around Dallas and Ft. Worth, figuring to give whoever was tailing me a tour of the town. I hoped he had a sense of humor.

Evening and the appointed hour arrived, so I freshened up and headed for the meeting room. I was greeted at the door by a large, rather well-muscled gentleman who looked more like a bodyguard than a greeter.

The man examined my invitation and gave me a once-over. "Mr. Dunn, there's a place for you at the table over to the left," he said with a nod I that direction.

There were only three tables with six seats at each, so the table to my left was hard to miss. By rough count, there were six gentlemen and three women already in attendance. I recognized none of them. They were exceedingly well-dressed, so I presumed that they were among the wealthy of Dallas. As a lawman, I found myself prone to make rather quick judgments of people. While there was a feel of tempered excitement among the guests I viewed, I sensed a hint of the dark underbelly that manifested in greed. These folks looked to be chafing at the bit to grow their wealth, and oil must have been their elixir.

Just as I was despairing of knowing anyone in the gathering, Colin O'Neal strode in. He wore a black suit with white shirt and blue cravat. It served to make him appear rather sinister but in a sophisticated sort of way. The nods he was receiving from guests appeared to be deferential. That seemed to belie his role as likely hired gun for Gordon Murphy.

A couple of more guests filtered into the room and everyone moved to their assigned seats. I introduced myself to the gentleman on my left and woman to my right. We made mostly meaningless conversation about the weather, the economy, and what the Spanish were up to that had our government in a twist. It was rumored that atrocities in Cuba had been exaggerated in the press. With the blowing up of the USS Maine in Havana Harbor, the Spanish-American War lit the fires of colonial expansion, resulting in the United States paying Spain twenty million dollars to reign as protector over Cuba, Puerto Rico, Guam, and the Philippines. The table discussion of the aftermath of the war focused on the opportunity it presented for the Texas economy to flourish. Black gold was expected to be a big part of the coming boom.

"What do you think of Theodore Roosevelt's ambitions, Mr. Dunn?" asked Mrs. Haskell between bites of steak.

"He is indeed an ambitious fellow," I responded noncommittally. I stole a glance toward the gentleman on my left, but he was animatedly engaged with another fellow beside him. There was no escaping Mrs. Haskell.

"Well, I think he fancies himself to be president," she persisted. "Do you agree?"

I was about to answer and was relieved when I saw O'Neal stride to a lectern placed at one end of the room. All conversation ceased.

O'Neal cleared his throat and scanned the room. "Welcome. It is good to see all of you again. I presume that means you are prepared to invest in the Dallas Oil Company." The man had a thick Irish accent. "At the center of each table, there is a prospectus for each of you. You have until Friday Noon to sign it and return it to me with an initial draft of fifty thousand dollars." The Irish mobster paused to permit his audience to digest his announcement. This had apparently been discussed at a previous meeting and was now coming to fruition. Assuming everyone signed on, this Dallas Oil Company would be taking in a handsome eight hundred fifty thousand dollars. "Are there any questions?"

A hand went up.

"Yes, Mr. Rollins," said O'Neal with an expression that suggested Rollins was a pain in his posterior.

Rollins stood. He was a rough-hewn man of perhaps forty-five years, during which he likely ranched and tilled a bit of soil. "Exactly where are the first drillings to occur?" asked Rollins.

O'Neal emitted an exasperated expression as though having had to endure these questions previously. "That information is in the prospectus, Mr. Rollins."

"I don't read too well, Mr. O'Neal. Can't you say?" persisted Rollins.

O'Neal glanced at the hired muscle still standing at the doorway. Fifty thousand dollars was fifty thousand dollars, so he'd endure Mr. Rollins for now. "Our first wells will be about twenty-five miles southeast of Corsicana."

Rollins sat.

"I see that we have a newcomer in our midst," noted O'Neal with a forced smile. "Mr. Dunn is a successful rancher and former lawman from down near Corpus Christi. Have you any questions, Mr. Dunn?"

I stood. "I may have a question or two after I review the prospectus. Thank you kindly."

"Just look us up," he responded. "I think you know where our office is," he said with a knowing smile that said his boss would love to catch me alone and have a go with knives. Undoubtedly, Murphy still bore the physical and mental scars of our previous encounter.

Thus far, it appeared that my money was as good as anyone else's. The suggestive photograph of me and the bar girl likely gave Murphy a bit of insurance against me causing him any difficulties.

The gathering began to break up. As I turned to leave, Mrs. Haskell grabbed my arm and gave me a confidential sort of look. "We're the first investors in Dallas Oil Company. I understand that there's a group like this in Houston and another in Austin." While it raised red flags for me, she seemed quite taken with the prospect of additional pools of big money investing in oil.

"That's right nice, Mrs. Haskell. Hopefully, we'll all earn a sweet return on our investment in the Dallas Oil Company." I nodded politely to indicate that our conversation was ended. About the time I reached the door, Murphy's security barred my exit.

His jaw was set in a neck about as wide as his shoulders. "Mr. O'Neal would have a brief word with you, sir."

I'm a tall, muscular man and capable of handling myself in any sort of brawl, but I had no desire to tangle with Murphy's hired muscle. I still reckoned they'd send McClintock after me once their oil game was running full bore here in Texas. I stood aside and permitted the last couple of attendees to leave.

O'Neal eased up alongside me. "It was a pleasure to have you join us this evening, Mr. Dunn. Please do stop by our office at your earliest convenience." He possessed one of those demeanors that begged to be challenged.

I kept my composure. I couldn't help thinking this invitation was more of a command than a passing suggestion. I caught the hired muscle's stoic expression. "I'll be sure to," I responded. "I assume y'all are interested in my fifty-thousand-dollar contribution."

O'Neal raised his eyebrows. I could swear that his tongue darted in and out like the snake he obviously was. With his nod to the hired muscle, I was permitted to exit.

There were no notes under my door, when I arrived at my room. Actually, there was more than that. The young lady from Corsicana was lying stark naked on my bed. She left nothing to the imagination so far as her appearance or intentions.

I stood frozen for a moment, collecting my thoughts. "You are a beautiful young lady, miss, but you can get dressed and leave."

"But I was paid to..." Her words trailed off, as she found her clothes tossed in her lap.

"Go!" I commanded and pointed toward the door.

She pouted but dressed. Even with clothes on, much of her smooth white flesh was revealed. She continued to pout, as she flounced herself from my room.

I locked the door behind her for what that was worth. I stripped down and climbed into the bed. There was the residual aroma of the young lady's perfume. Hard to ignore, but I sure try. As I laid back on the bed and thought on the past couple of days, I reckoned I was on a business gusher of sorts. I figured to sleep with my Smith & Wesson under my pillow.

ELEVEN
FIGHTING WORDS

I CLIMBED two flights of stairs to Murphy's office suite. Coincidentally, the address duplicated the address on the Dallas Oil Company prospectus. How interesting. In fact, my visit was made even more interesting by seeing my beloved banker Mr. Carson, scurrying away from Murphy's office. With a long tail, he'd easily be mistaken for a large rat. Luckily, he hadn't noticed my arrival at the opposite end of the corridor.

I waited to be certain Carson was gone, then knocked on the office door. I heard steps approach. None other than Murphy's hired muscle opened the door just enough to see into the dimly lit hall. He swung the door wider. "Mr. Dunn is here, sir," he announced.

I stepped in and found Gordon Murphy walking toward me with a hand extended. Other than the brief passing in the hotel restaurant a couple of days earlier, I hadn't rested my eyes on Gordon Murphy again until this moment. As we shook hands, I couldn't help but notice the nasty-looking scar that decorated his hand, thanks to the last time he tussled with me. "Welcome to Dallas Oil, Mr.

Dunn." He said in a vain attempt to sound warmly welcoming.

"Why, thank you, Mr. Murphy. I've had a chance to review the prospectus that Mr. O'Neal so kindly provided and reckoned to stop by your offices to sign copies and offer my bank draft." I glanced about and noted that Murphy had spared no expense in creating a right upscale office setting for this supposedly fledgling endeavor. I wouldn't have been surprised if as much as half of the investment dollars were on their way to New York City, with a cut to some folks in Ireland proper.

"Do come and have a seat for a moment." He motioned to a chair near a highboy. "George, please fetch two copies of the prospectus."

So, the hired muscle's name was George. It sounded innocent enough. I watched him lumber away to a back office.

"I'm sorry that Mr. O'Neal isn't available to join us. He's off on company business," excused Murphy.

I suspected he was raising money from another set of gullible monied folks whose yearning for quick riches exceeded their rational judgment. "The prospectus doesn't mention a specific site. Do you have a specific location in mind?" I figured to goad him a little by repeating Mr. Rollins' question from the hotel gathering.

Murphy failed to react, but I saw George flinch as he came back into the office.

George placed the prospectus copies before Murphy and me, along with documents to facilitate money transfer. As he turned, he purposely brushed my arm with just enough force to remind me that he was a force. I had the urge to stretch my leg out in front of him as he passed and watch him fall clumsily on his face. I kept myself in check. I turned to Murphy. "The site?" I repeated.

"Er...little place called Richmond. It's south of Corsicana." Murphy seemed just a bit evasive.

"I know where Richmond is. Y'all think there's oil there?" I pressed.

"It's a chancy business as you surely know, Mr. Dunn." He tried to sound reassuring.

I couldn't contain a patronizing smile. "A gamble indeed," I observed. I took a few moments in a deafening silence to review the additional papers. "These documents seem to be in order, Mr. Murphy," I finally told him.

"Feel free to call me Gordon," he responded.

The suggestion took me off guard. I hadn't anticipated getting casual with this lawbreaking scum. "Sure enough, Gordon. You can call me Luke."

Murphy leaned forward. "Well, Luke, if I learn that you are in any way looking to make trouble for me and the Dallas Oil Company, I will permit George here to show you how turncoats are dealt with in New York City. Do I make myself clear?"

What was I to say? "I'm sorry that you harbor any doubts as to my intentions, Gordon. I look forward to a successful investment outcome."

George folded his arms across his chest and looked as though he'd like nothing better than to tear me apart with his bare hands.

I wondered whether George was as agile as he was large. Murphy and I signed the papers and I provided a bank draft against my funds in the Dallas Trust. I reckoned that Mr. Carson would be pleased to handle that. "What's next, Gordon?"

Murphy leaned back in his chair. "With the animosity of your recent separation from the Texas Rangers, might we coax you into serving as a set of eyes for us. We don't appreciate the law breathing down our necks as it were."

Now, we were getting into why Murphy wanted me to physically visit his office. He wanted a safe setting to propose a role for me in his organization. Unbeknownst to him, it would place me in the position of being a double agent. "Let me think on that, Gordon."

"Do let us know in the next day or so," he said with an eye to George, indicating some persuasion might be in order. He leveled his eyes on me atop a diabolical smile. "Did you enjoy Miss Lilly?"

"Not so I can recall," I responded. "Lovely young lady, but I'm sure you know that. I believe you might even possess proof."

Murphy smiled at my reference to the compromising photograph. "Your wife's name is Cassie, isn't it?"

My eyes flashed from Murphy to George and back. "Let me be clear. Regardless of any arrangement we have, you harm her and you're both dead men. Is that clear?"

Murphy shook off my threat and stood. "Think on my offer, Luke."

George escorted me to the office exit door. "Don't cross him," he advised with a low, gravelly voice as he let me out. He gave me a parting steely-eyed glower that said he'd love to whip me to within inches of my life. Little wonder the Irish Mob was ruling the neighborhoods in New York City, if this was the sort of influence they brought to bear.

I nodded with a polite smile that wordlessly told him I'd welcome the opportunity. I wasn't about to be put down by the likes of this thug.

I suppose I was, technically speaking, a de facto part of the Irish Mob. The transition had been easier than I'd expected. In fact, it had been too easy.

What to do next? Talk to investors from other gatherings similar to that at the Union Depot Hotel? Visit Richmond? I supposed that I could lead whoever was tailing me on a merry chase across Texas.

I decided to begin with Mrs. Haskell.

The talkative hotel desk clerk was his usual helpful self and told me where I might find the lady. He shared that her husband had vast holdings in cattle and cotton. He was looking to expand into the oil business and had put Mrs. Haskell to work pursuing that effort. I suppose that it was quite a shift from managing fields of cotton and cattle ranges to the financing of oil exploration.

I obtained a horse from the livery near the hotel and headed out to the Haskell spread. The place was impressive. This was the cattle portion of Haskell's empire. I reckoned that the cotton part of his business was further to the south. A white picket fence surrounded an unimposing two-story frame ranch house with four stately Georgian columns across a wide veranda. I hitched my mount, dismounted, and climbed the four steps leading to the front door. At my first knock, I heard light footsteps. The door opened, and I found myself facing a young Black woman in a maid's uniform.

"May I help you, sir?"

"Why yes. My name is Lucas Dunn, and I'd like to chat with Mr. and Mrs. Haskell."

She gave me a once-over. "Please step inside, Mr. Dunn, and wait here in the foyer. I'll see whether either is available." She paused. "What is the nature of your business?"

"Oil. I wish to talk about oil exploration," I replied. I observed that she was well-spoken and polite enough. She must have dealt with unexpected visitors a time or two.

The young woman returned a few moments later. "Please follow me."

I fell in behind her, as she led me to a library a few steps from the foyer.

"Please make yourself comfortable, Mr. Dunn. Mr. Haskell is away, but Mrs. Haskell will be along shortly." She shut the door behind her and left me to my thoughts and hundreds of books.

The library was what I might call small but mighty. The books spanned just about every known genre and included classics as well as nonfiction science and history works. A copy of a biography of Theodore Roosevelt lay open on a side table near an easy chair. I suppose that had prompted her questioning about Roosevelt's ambitions.

The door swung open and Mrs. Haskell swept into the room. She wore a green brocade dress that set off her red hair, which fell over her shoulders. She might best be described as a handsome woman as opposed to beautiful. She'd undoubtedly been quite a catch in an earlier life. Now, money had become a substitute for youth. "Why, Mr. Dunn. How nice of you to visit. Had I known you were coming, I'd have been better prepared." She swept her hands over her dress as though it were unsuitable.

"I apologize for any inconvenience, Mrs. Haskell. I'm also sorry that your husband is unavailable."

She laughed. "Well, whether you're here about Theodore Roosevelt or oil or both, it's just as well. Claude's not interested in either." She slipped over to a coffee service. "Care for coffee?"

I nodded. "I visited with Mr. O'Neal's boss yesterday," I ventured, as I accepted a steaming cup of coffee.

"Do you speak of Mr. Murphy? Interesting fellow. Irish, I gather." She motioned me to the twin of the easy chair with the Roosevelt biography. "Those Irish have quite a strange accent," she observed.

"He and I had a conversation. Seems they plan to drill in Richmond."

"Richmond? I'd understood they'd be drilling closer to Houston," she said with a curiously uncertain expression.

"It's an uncertain business, Mrs. Haskell."

"If I'm not being too inquisitive, have you invested?" she asked.

"Yes. Yes, I have." I took a sip of coffee and observed her reaction.

She blinked. "I've been talking with some friends in Houston who are considering investment in this Dallas Oil Company venture."

"And?" I pressed.

"They want to see derricks and drilling before they'll invest. You might call it a proof of good faith."

Mrs. Haskell was no dummy as concerned financial matters. I would likely have felt the same way if I were investing my own money rather than that of the Texas government. While my investment would be held to account, Haskell's was at considerable risk. "I understand. It's certainly wise of you."

Mrs. Haskell leaned forward and lowered her voice. "Can I be brutally honest with you, Mr. Dunn? For some reason, I feel that I can trust you, and I'm in a bit of a quandary."

"I have no axe to grind here, Mrs. Haskell. Anything you say will be held in confidence." I took another sip of coffee in an attempt to appear relaxed, though I had suddenly become quite excited at the prospect of some secret being revealed.

Mrs. Haskell drew a slip of paper from a side pocket in her dress and handed it to me. "It arrived yesterday."

I read the note slowly and carefully. The Irish Mob was flaunting its influence over the cotton trade in New York

City. If the Haskells wished to continue selling their cotton to New York buyers, an investment in the Dallas Oil Company was strongly suggested. "When did you receive this?" I asked.

"Last night. My husband doesn't know about it yet," replied Mrs. Haskell.

"Are you going to invest?" I asked.

"I'm scared not to, Mr. Dunn. And I'm fearful of telling my husband what I've gotten us into," she lamented.

"Do you know other folks who've been similarly threatened?"

"I haven't had the opportunity to talk with the other investors. I'm afraid to use the telephone, as someone might be listening in."

"You're right smart about that, ma'am," I said. It didn't surprise me that the Irish Mob was resorting to extortion. Whether or not they actually did any oil exploration was of secondary concern to Murphy and his handlers back east. I wished I could reassure Mrs. Haskell by revealing my involvement, but it was imperative that I maintain my cover.

"You might contact Deputy US Marshal Miller," I suggested.

"I'm frightened that they'll do worse, if I go to the law," said Mrs. Haskell with fear emblazoned across her face. She began to tremble.

"You may be right. Still, I can't believe that they will ultimately succeed at this, Mrs. Haskell. Somebody will surely be bold enough to step forward." I wanted to comfort her, but dared not get intimate. "If I hear of any other investors facing the same threat and they're willing to come forward, I'll let you know." I wasn't very reassuring, and that was frustrating for me.

"I would deeply appreciate anything you can do, Mr. Dunn."

"Well, I'm planning on visiting Richmond in the next few days to see what sort of progress, if any, is being made. If you wouldn't mind sharing the names of other investors, I'd be pleased to visit them." I reckoned that I just might find a soul brave enough to step up against Murphy.

"I can give you a list of five whom my husband and I are acquainted with," she responded. She promptly took a pad from a drawer of the sideboy and began making a list. After a few quiet moments, she handed it to me. "You did not get this here, Mr. Dunn."

"Be assured that the source is safe with me," I replied. "Well, I'd best be on my way. Thank you for your hospitality."

She smiled. "You never did answer my question about Theodore Roosevelt's ambitions."

"You've got me there, ma'am. I'm afraid that I don't know enough about the man and can only say that I believe he is ambitious. Perhaps it's enough to seek higher office."

She smiled as though somewhat satisfied. "I'll see you to the door. Thank you for hearing me out."

I found my way back to my horse and headed back to town.

☆☆

As I rounded a bend in the road, I couldn't help but notice a black horse-drawn surrey parked beneath a live oak. Especially noticeable were the driver and his passenger. I asked myself what the hell Karl Aimes was doing with Murphy's muscle man, George? What could the mayor's assistant possibly be thinking?

"Mr. Dunn," called out George. "Do come chat with us."

I likely could have easily ridden off, but what was the point? They'd eventually find me. I rode over to their rig.

"How was your visit with Mrs. Haskell?" asked Aimes.

This had the trappings of looking like an ugly situation. What was it to them if I visited Mrs. Haskell? "It was friendly. Nice to know that I'm popular enough for my activities to be followed." I forced a confident smile.

"How about climbing down from that bronc, so we can have a discussion about your visit?" asked George as he began to remove his shirt. His upper body rippled with muscles on top of muscles.

"Are you sure you want to have this discussion?" I queried.

"The fewer words the better," said George.

I looked at Aimes. "Does Mayor Woods know about the sandbox you're playing in, Mr. Aimes?" What was he doing so far from Corsicana?

"What he don't know can't hurt him," responded Aimes. He seemed about as slimy a critter as could be conjured up.

George seemed put off. "Say, this is about you being with Mrs. Haskell. Leave the mayor out of it." He puffed out his enormous chest. "This is where I teach you a lesson, Mr. Dunn." His lips went wide with one of the evilest smiles I'd ever seen.

"Well, I reckoned it would eventually come to this. Allow me to remove my jacket and hang up my gun." I dawdled a bit, as I made a show of hanging my gun rig over my saddle horn. "I expect that Mr. Aimes here knows a good doctor in town to take you to."

George blinked then shook his head and repeated his dastardly smile. "Think this is funny, do you?"

I glanced at Aimes. "Is there room in the back of that rig for a body?"

George had had enough. Like a bull, he charged at me.

I stepped aside but caught his ankle with my boot as he flew past.

He fell flat on his face.

"They hold folks back east so they can't move?" I taunted.

He hauled his great bulk up to a standing position and spat out a bit of dust. His front side was covered in trail dust. Beneath the grime, his face and upper body grew red with rage. Instead of rushing at me, he stepped purposefully forward and began a roundhouse right punch, which I neatly ducked while my knee caught him in the groin. George graveled on the ground, doubled over in pain. "You damned sonofabitch!" he growled between groans. He once again managed to get to his feet.

As he wobbled a moment, I stepped in and crushed a left jab into his nose. It landed with a resounding crack, and blood spurted across his face.

He staggered back a step with his hand over his broken snout.

Just as I was about to follow my jab with a finishing right, all went blank. From what I'd figure later, something caught the back of my head and leveled me out. It was likely Aimes, but I'll never be sure.

I came to in my hotel room bed. My ribs were killing me, but soothing fingers were applying cool compresses to my aching head. My eyes fluttered open, and I focused them on none other than Lilly.

"Oh, good. You're awake," she cooed. "The men who brought you here said you'd had a nasty fall from your horse. You're lucky it wasn't any worse." She gently raised my head to fluff my pillow. That put her cleavage within an inch of my nose.

The smell of her perfume lingered. "Who brought me here?"

"Mayor Woods' assistant brought me here to nurse you. I don't know who brought you here."

If she leaned across me again, she'd be nursing me all right, but from her ample chest. I was hurting too much to give a damn. "Thanks for…" I realized that I was stark naked under the blanket.

Lilly gave me a pouty smile as she recognized what I'd suddenly become aware of. "Shame you're a man of such high and mighty principles, Mr. Dunn. I'd love to…well, you know what I'd love to do." She changed the compress on my forehead.

Her soothing touch returned me to drowsiness, and I fell back to sleep.

I awakened next morning and painfully managed to swing my legs off the side of the bed. I stared into the mirror ahead of me. One eye had bruises around it, and my ribs still hurt like hell. A couple of ribs were likely broken or just shy of that. There was no evidence of Lilly's visit. I wouldn't have been surprised if they had made further use of photography upon stripping off my clothes and dumping me into the bed. I couldn't worry about it.

It was small solace that I'd been putting a serious whupping on George when my lights were turned off. Knowing that I'd busted his nose, I took some comfort in knowing that he, too, was feeling pain. In a perverse sort of way, I looked forward to meeting up with him again.

I reached for my jacket and fished out the notepaper

with the list of investors that Mrs. Haskell had provided. I decided to look them up before heading to Richmond. It would be interesting to see what sort of consequence Murphy would throw at me next. I'd give even money that George would demur even under pressure from Murphy. Worst case, Mr. Muscle might resort to a weapon.

There wasn't too much I could do about my injuries. I got myself shaved and dressed as best I could. I had breakfast sent up to my room.

I finally stepped out from the hotel into a sunny day with the front brim of my hat tipped low to hide my bruised eye as much as possible. As I headed up toward the livery stables, I passed none other but my dear banker, Mr. Carson.

"You okay this morning, Mr. Dunn. Hear tell one of Pulaski's horses dumped you." He was a tad too smug for my liking. His fat cheeks shook when he spoke, giving him the overall appearance of a bowl of jelly.

It was amazing how quickly tales could spread. "Spooked by a rattler, thank you," I responded. I reckoned that I might as well keep up the ruse. I watched the fat rat roll away toward the bank. I soon found myself at the livery.

"Yuh gonna give one of my hosses another chance?" asked the stableboy.

"Actually, I'd be pleased to use the same horse," I insisted.

He shook his head, as he ambled off to fetch the gray stallion. He emerged a few minutes later with the horse in tow.

"Looks pretty docile to me," I stated.

The stable boy had no idea what *docile* meant.

"Calm. Gentle," I explained.

"Well, have a good ride," he said as he handed the reins to me.

Off I rode.

Well, I visited with a Mr. Ross and a Mr. Nettles. Both lived in rather palatial ranch houses, leaving little doubt as to how they'd amassed their fortunes. Conversations with each were similar to that with Mrs. Haskell, and both would come forward if someone else came forward first. The extortion scheme was consistently diabolical.

The good news for me was that I saw nothing of Aimes or of George. That left me to wonder what Murphy was cooking up. He surely knew of my visits. I also wondered how O'Neal was making out, making his investor pitches and then extorting the money from folks too embarrassed to turn the gang in.

It seemed to me that they would set up a minimum of activity in Richmond in case inquisitive folks like myself wanted to verify that the Dallas Oil Company was a going concern.

TWELVE
RICHMOND SCAM

I TOOK the train to Corsicana, then secured a horse to take me to Richmond. So far as I could tell, Murphy's spy was not on my tail. He must have decided that he had enough on me to keep me harmlessly under his thumb.

I made my way to the Exchange Hotel. As I rode up to the hitching rail, I noted the adjoining facilities where slave trading used to take place. The aftermath of that time in history still raised its ugly head. My dad used to tell me of all he'd dealt with during the War Between the States. Places like Richmond, Texas, could never outlive the association with slavery. The local government had likely welcomed the prospect of Gordon Murphy bringing new opportunity to the town in the form of oil.

"Where might I find the Dallas Oil Company operations?" I asked the desk clerk.

He gave me a sour look. It was my first hint that folks in Richmond might not be pleased with the oil operations. "Over thataway," he pointed. "'Bout an hour ride toward the lake."

"Much obliged," I responded and signed the register.

"Yuh part of thet oil outfit?"

"An investor. Reckoned to check it out."

He gave me a strange look. "Not much tuh see, mistuh."

"You say about an hour ride?" I glanced outside to reassure myself that there'd be enough light to ride to the oil field and return to the hotel before dark. I stowed my satchel in my room and headed out to the Dallas Oil Company site.

The site wasn't hard to find. There was a gateway arch emblazoned with the company name. Beyond were five oil derricks lying about on their sides like carrion. There were no drill bits and no casings to be seen. I chuckled to myself. The Irish Mob was nothing if not sloppy. The folks back in New York City must have figured the people in Texas to have more money than sense. They looked on us as yokels, as unsophisticated backwoods folks to be easily duped.

There was no point in hanging around the supposed oil field, so I headed back to the Exchange Hotel. It was high time that I began bringing Murphy's scheme to an end.

I mounted up and headed back toward Corsicana first thing in the morning. The day was clear, and I figured I could catch the afternoon train to Dallas. The ride gave me plenty of time to mull over exactly how I would bring down Murphy's house of cards.

A bullet buzzed past my ear. I dove for cover, sore ribs and all, and managed to pull the Smith & Wesson from my holster as I reached the only tree in sight. Silence. I heard the faint sound of a lever action and another bullet zoomed past in my general direction. If I had to take a wild guess, Kyle McClintock was after me again. I thanked God that he was a poor marksman. "Damn McClintock! Are you crazy?" I shouted.

"Who you callin' crazy?" hollered a voice. It wasn't McClintock.

I was in a bit of a jam. The Smith & Wesson revolver is a superb firearm, but it was tough going against a rifle. Whoever it was shooting at me could rain lead from a greater distance and just might get lucky. My cayuse was standing about a hundred yards off. Could I chance a run for it? My good sense told me to sit tight. The bushwhacker might lose patience and make a mistake. In my experience and from what my Texas Ranger dad told me, those who took up the gun for hire eventually made a mistake that doomed them. Maybe, this fellow's time had come. I just sat there quietly awaiting the gunman's next move. A couple of bullets ricocheted harmlessly off the trunk of the tree.

This was a stalemate for the moment. If the bushwhacker was smart, he'd back off and go set another ambush up the road somewhere. Did I say *if he was smart*? Another bullet grazed the tree trunk. I heard a chafing of denim and knock of a boot heel against a rock. It sounded as though my attacker was moving. I removed my hat and peeked out toward where I'd figured he'd begun his ambush. I saw the top of his hat and heard him lever another round into his receiver. He'd roughly halved the distance between us. My suspicion that he wasn't so smart seemed to be correct.

He sent another bullet my way. I peeked again. He was about a hundred and fifty feet away. It was still not close enough to bring my Smith & Wesson into play. I looked up over my head. There was a branch about six feet above ground that looked as though it could support my weight. The tree trunk was broad enough that I just might be able to climb to the branch for a bird's eye view of the bushwhacker. Importantly, if he closed on me, he wouldn't expect me to be above him. I holstered my gun and prepared to climb up to the branch.

The ambusher fired off two rounds in quick succession.

I screamed as though hit. "My God, you've killed me!" I shouted then scrambled up to the branch. It bent slightly under my weight but held me. I unholstered my revolver and waited for the bushwhacker to investigate his kill.

If he'd looked up, he might have spotted me.

He approached cautiously to within ten feet of the tree. When he realized that I wasn't bleeding out behind the tree, a bewildered expression crossed his face.

"Up here," I said.

He lifted the muzzle of his carbine too slowly. I placed three neat holes in the man, one in the belly and two more in his chest as he dropped. He was barely alive as he hit the ground.

I scrambled from my perch and approached the man. "Who sent your sorry ass?" I asked to no avail.

He opened his mouth but never got any words out.

I searched his pockets. Stuffed inside his jacket was a bundle of hundred-dollar bills in a paper wrapper from the Dallas Trust. I stuffed the money in my pocket. I found a photograph of the dead man with a worn-out-looking woman and three children. Scrawled on the back was a name nearly obliterated by time and wear. The name looked to be Stanton. I made a note of it and placed the photograph back into the man's pocket. I wondered what must have driven Mr. Stanton so low in life and now death? I reckoned that he had a horse tethered somewhere close by, so I fetched mine and eventually found his. I tied Stanton over his saddle and headed toward Corsicana. I figured to drop him off with Sheriff Allen.

To be straight, I rather wished the bushwhacker had been McClintock.

I had confirmed that the Dallas Oil Company's Richmond Field was a ruse, a scam, a put-up job. But for a few derricks, there hadn't even appeared to be any intention of drilling. So where were the investment dollars going? I reckoned that the answer lay with the Dallas Trust and some folks in New York City raking in a heady take of Texas money.

I knew nothing about the sheriff in Navarro County. What sort of man was Bob Allen? Could he be trusted? Here I was bringing in a man I'd killed, and the sheriff would have every right to arrest me. I couldn't tell him that I was a Texas Ranger working undercover with the US Marshal's Office to bring down the efforts of the Irish Mob to set up their operations in Texas.

I decided that discretion made the best sense. I waited until dark, rode into Corsicana, and hitched the horse carrying Stanton's body to the hitching post in front of the jail. I wrote a note to the effect that the victim was a bushwhacker who'd failed at his task and to please forward the man's personal effects to his family. Sheriff Allen would find it in the morning.

I returned my mount to the livery, grabbed my satchel from the stableboy, and strolled up the street toward the train depot. As I passed the Iron Front Saloon, I heard raucous laughter. I was figuring to spend the night on a rock-hard bench at the train depot, so a whiskey or two might ease the aches and pains I faced. Besides, my sore ribs occasionally reminded me of their presence, and the bench wouldn't ease the hurt.

I walked through the batwing doors and paused. But for a couple of gentlemen at the far end of the bar, the noise continued. I caught sight of jaws dropping on the two whose attention I'd attracted. It was as though they'd seen a ghost. As I sidled up to the bar, the two men scurried from the saloon. My intuition kicked in, as I suspected they'd be reporting to Murphy that Lucas Dunn still lived. I leaned back against the bar. Scanning the room, I saw Lilly entertaining a couple of clients at the far end. She was too busy with her prospects than to notice me.

Standing at the bar, sipping a whiskey that warmed my innards, turned out to be a good thing. It enabled me to bring all I knew into sharper focus. It appeared as though I now had to be extra cautious, as it was clear that Murphy had decided that my being a threat outweighed any usefulness. The money trail was critically important, and I judged the Dallas Trust to be in the thick of it. The investment money would be deposited in the bank, the bank would clean it up—launder it, as you will—through various accounts and send some portion to New York City and some to Gordon Murphy. Yes, a visit with Ernest Carson looked to be in order.

I quaffed my whiskey but decided against another and headed out to the train depot. Walking toward the depot took me past the jail. The horse with Stanton's body draped over its saddle was still hitched. I admit to feeling a pang of remorse that I couldn't personally hand over the body to Sheriff Allen.

The train depot was deserted. I got to thinking on the two men who'd hastily departed the Iron Front Saloon upon my arrival. Maybe, it wasn't such a good idea to spend the night sleeping on a depot bench. Given Stanton's failure, someone else may be assigned to the job. The loft at the livery seemed a better choice given the circumstances.

Besides, the hay would make for a considerably more comfortable bed.

I bought my passage back to Dallas first thing in the morning. There were no suspicious-looking folks lingering around the depot. An early departure found me in a warm, dry passenger car looking out at gray skies, misty rain, and muddy streets. I wondered whether Sheriff Allen had yet discovered the gift I left for him.

By now, Murphy surely must have known that his assassin had failed. I figured I'd learn more upon arrival in Dallas. In a perverse sort of way, I relished the prospect.

THIRTEEN
DALLAS TRUST

THE TRAIN RIDE from Corsicana was uneventful. If I were still being followed, there certainly was no evidence of it. Murphy had likely become overconfident. If so, it would lead to his downfall.

With a great hissing of steam and squealing of brakes, the train pulled into the Dallas train depot. As the train came to a halt and I began to rise from my seat, a passenger strode by and dropped a piece of paper on my seat. I glanced at what appeared to be a note and then the backside of the passenger, as she disappeared out the rear door of the car.

Naturally, I picked up the note and read it. "Leave on side opposite platform." It was short and sweet. Was it from friend or foe? Could this be a setup for an ambush? I drew my Smith & Wesson and checked the loads. With my free hand, I grabbed my satchel.

I paused before exiting the rear door of the car. The train would be pulling out in but a moment, so I had to make my decision. I headed through the door, turned as though about to exit opposite the platform, and then climbed down onto the depot platform. I scanned up and down the sightline afforded by the train. No bullets were flying. I made a beeline for the depot and arrived inside just as the train pulled from the station. If anyone had been lying in wait, they'd been disappointed.

I headed for the Union Depot Hotel across from the train depot. The street was busy. If someone was gunning for me, there was a lot of street clutter that would spoil their aim. I quickly found myself in front of the desk clerk.

"Welcome back, Mr. Dunn. We held your room, as you requested."

"Thanks kindly. Have I had any visitors?" I asked.

"Not since a few days back when you had that unfortunate fall from your horse."

He reminded me that while the bruise around my eye had cleared, my ribs remained a tad sore. "Please arrange a hot bath," I requested. It simply made good sense to be cleaned up from my travels before visiting Carson.

Upon reaching the stairway landing, I peered to my left up the hall toward my room. I caught the reflection of a sunbeam on blued steel and hit the deck just as the blast from a shotgun swept over me.

I yanked my gun as I rolled and opened fire at the source of the blast. I heard my first two bullets hit flesh. By my third shot, I heard a grunt and the thud of a body hitting the floor. The sound of running footsteps reached me from downstairs, as the desk clerk ran for the sheriff. The hall was thick with the acrid odor of gun smoke, such that I was unable to see to the end where a body surely lay. I heard a moan and a raspy gurgle. From experience, the bushwhacker was either dead or close to it. I looked to the wall on my right. There wasn't much to be said for its condition, thanks to what was likely ten-gauge shot.

As the gun smoke cleared and quiet arose from the

shooter's end of the hall, I finally reckoned it was safe to stand. I could now make out an inert form lying on the floor at the end of the hallway. I heard steps behind me and turned to see Sheriff Moon approaching with a frightened desk clerk standing at the base of the stairway.

"What's happened here?" asked Moon. Tough, politically savvy sheriff that he was, Moon behaved as though this wasn't his first rodeo.

"I dodged a shotgun blast and returned fire, Sheriff. I haven't checked on the man behind the shotgun yet, but far as I can see through the gun smoke, he looks to be dead."

"Give me your sidearm and stay here," ordered Moon.

I extended the gun to him butt first.

Moon took my Smith & Wesson and strode up the hall toward the man lying unmoving on the floor. He kneeled down to confirm that the man was dead.

He came back to me and looked me in the eyes. "Looks to be that you're telling the truth." He examined my gun. "You hit him three of four shots. Not bad for blind shooting." He handed the gun back to me. "The man is a local ne'er-do-well. Likely hired to kill you," he observed. "You're Luke Dunn, aren't you?" he finally asked.

"Yes," I replied.

It was obvious that he'd heard of my falling out with the Texas Rangers. "You'd best be watching your backside, Dunn. From what I hear, you're mixing with a rough crowd." He peered down the stairwell at the desk clerk. "I'll send somebody to clean this up. You can go about your business." He turned back to me. "He's a good kid, but overly curious."

"I expect that I won't be here much longer, Sheriff. I'll try not to make further trouble." I tried to be reassuring, knowing it was impossible.

Moon simply shook his head and departed. "You be careful," were his parting words of advice.

I reloaded my revolver. Curious and with the smoke mostly cleared, I walked down the hall to the dead man. He lay on his back in a pool of blood. I confirmed that my shooting had indeed been right fine. With that, I entered my room to wait for my bath.

Life in Dallas had surely become tenuous. I was determined to visit Ernest Carson. After the two recent attempts on my life, I was of a mind to make the fat pig sweat some.

The desk clerk got himself together enough to order a bath for me. Refreshed from my travels and two attempts on my life, I dressed appropriate to meeting a banker. I double-checked the load in my Smith & Wesson.

I cautiously opened the door, checked left and right, and eventually slipped out the back door of the hotel and into the dim light of dusk.

September was nearly in the books, and the daylight hours would be ever fewer. A bit of a chill had settled on the town, as I headed for Carson's abode. I didn't reckon to meet him in his lair at the bank, so I bribed the desk clerk to get me Carson's address. I stuck mostly to alleys and stayed clear of the gas lamps. There was no point in making it easy for any lurking bushwhackers.

Carson's home was lit up like a Christmas tree. Lights seemed to be ablaze in just about every window. From the appearance of the two-story Georgian-style frame structure, the banker was not hurting for money. Looking into the window of the dining room, Carson was seated with a woman who was likely his wife and four children. I'd never considered whether the man had a family. I decided to wait until dinner was finished and then do what I could to get Carson alone. I kept my eye on that dining room gathering, but from a distance.

Finally, Carson leveraged his weight against the table and stood. He rubbed his belly and smiled at his wife and children. He grabbed a cigar from a humidor and headed out the back door to a gazebo where he ensconced himself on a pillowed bench. He drew a cigar from his pocket and was soon sending smoke spiraling skyward.

I emerged from a bush beside the gazebo with my revolver in hand. "Good evening, Ernest. Let's you and me take a little walk," I suggested.

Carson's eyes went huge with surprise. "D-D-Dunn!" he croaked, half swallowing his cigar.

"Yep. That's me, Ernest. Now climb your fat ass down here and let's walk."

Carson moved his hand toward a vest pocket.

The metallic clicking sound as I pulled back my hammer brought him up short. "Don't be stupid, Ernest. The sound from my Smith & Wesson and your scream of pain as my bullet plowed through your gut would alert your family. I'm sure they'd mourn your demise."

Carson sighed and moved his hand away from his vest pocket. The banker lifted his considerable girth from the bench and waddled down the gazebo steps. He stood nervously in front of me with beads of sweat beginning to appear on his brow.

I relieved him of his pocket pistol. I was surprised that his fat fingers could fit within the trigger guard. "Come with me. You're going to do some talking, Ernest."

"Who the hell are you to treat me like this, Dunn?" he asked.

"For now, let's just say that I'm a very concerned

investor." I nudged him along with my pistol. I sorely wanted to arrest the man.

We were finally at the edge of a stand of live oaks about a hundred yards from the house. "I've spoken with other investors and seen the sham of an oil operation in Richmond. Murphy seems to have some sort of threat hanging over each investor. What does Gordon Murphy hold over you?" I reckoned to get right to the crux of the situation.

Carson looked at me through the eyes of a dead man. "I can't tell you."

"No need. I can pretty much guess." Now, I stuck the muzzle of the Smith & Wesson under Carson's chin. A pull on the trigger, and his brains would be spread across half of Dallas. "Do you keep a ledger on your transactions for Murphy?" Sweat was bathing Carson's face, and the shirt under his armpits was soaking wet. I pressed the muzzle just a little harder into the underside of his chin.

"Y-y-y-yes," he responded nervously.

"This gun has a hair trigger. Where is this ledger?"

"My desk…in my house," he replied.

"Shut up, Carson," came a voice from behind me. I recognized it as Karl Aimes. The slithering snake had arrived at a highly inopportune time.

"Why, Karl, what brings you here on such a beautiful evening?" I said.

"Let him go or I'll shoot you dead," threatened Aimes.

"That doesn't sound like a fair outcome, Karl. Maybe you can help me here. I'd sure like to know how Mayor Woods plays into this?" I remained calm, as I asked the question. I think it threw Aimes off his game just a little.

"He ain't involved. Now step away from Ernest there," he demanded.

"You're at least fifty feet away, Karl. Do you really figure you can get in a kill shot before I lay you out dead?" My only chance was to work on his confidence.

I heard the click, as Aimes pulled back the hammer of his pistol.

With that, I ducked low and aimed carefully. My move caused Aimes to hesitate. I put a bullet dead center in his face. The booming report echoed through the night and brought Carson's wife and children to the gazebo. Carson stood frozen. Aimes lay stone still in a spreading pool of blood.

"Y'all go inside and be quiet," I called out. "Your pa is okay. I'll get the sheriff." Like hell I would.

"Ernest?" called his wife.

"I'm okay. Do as he says," replied Carson.

The family scurried back inside.

Carson was now sweating enough to flood the Brazos River. "M-m-my heart," he mumbled and dropped to his knees.

I didn't need a dead Ernest Carson on my hands. "Get a hold of yourself, Ernest. Imagine if I were Gordon Murphy holding this gun."

"What do you need?" pleaded Carson, as the color began to return to his face.

"The ledger. You give me the ledger, and I'll see that no harm befalls you."

"How can you be so sure?" pressed the banker.

"Your friend Murphy set his muscle on me and then two bushwhackers. George is still nursing his busted nose, and the two sent to kill me are pushing up daisies. I think I can be sure you'll be safe."

Carson began to breathe more easily. "Okay. Okay, I'll give you the ledgers."

"Put them in a bag and hide them behind that tree by tomorrow night," I said, pointing to a nearby live oak.

"Now, let's get you back to your after-dinner cigar." With that, I holstered my gun and sent Carson on his way.

I watched him wobble his way back to the gazebo. He plopped onto a bench and was subjected to his wife. She apparently scolded him, as she waved a pointed finger in his face. I reckoned Carson was getting all he deserved. If he turned witness for the state, he'd likely avoid jail but never run a bank again. If the Irish Mob found out about his duplicity, he'd likely be a dead man.

I strode over to Aimes' body. What a fool he was. I grabbed his collar and dragged him off the path. I figured to leave a note for Sheriff Moon. The poor lawman would be getting his fill of Luke Dunn.

As I headed back to the Union Depot Hotel, it occurred to me that I'd not seen or heard from Colin O'Neal. I assumed he was spewing his promises of making Texans wealthier through investment in black gold.

FOURTEEN
GEORGE ROUND TWO

I RECKONED my day was just about done. Having endured the ambusher near my room at the hotel, the short-lived threat from Karl Aimes, and dealing with Ernest Carson, I was bushed. My plan was to enter the hotel as I'd departed: through the back door. A full moon lit the scene with its silvery reflections. Shucks, it was akin to daylight. So it was that I couldn't miss a large, shadowy figure standing at the door. George.

"Mr. Murphy wants to see you," he growled.

"He can wait until tomorrow morning," I responded.

"He wants to see you now," demanded George.

"And I said tomorrow," I replied with authority.

"One way or another, you're coming with me," stated George firmly. He began to remove his shirt.

"Careful, George," I warned. "Karl Aimes isn't around to help you."

The implied insult caused the big man's face to redden. "I'll tear you apart, you damned sonofabitch." He took two steps toward me and found himself looking cross-eyed down the barrel of my .38 caliber Smith & Wesson. His eyes bulged, as he froze in place.

"Another step, and you'll be needing a new face, George. You want to test me?"

The big man's shoulders sagged with resignation. One of his bull rushes wouldn't end well for him. "You win, dammit," he groused.

I kept my gun aimed at him. "What's gotten into Murphy?" It was an open-ended question, and I reckoned that George might know enough to fill in any blanks if he was willing to talk. It was likely that keeping his own mouth shut kept him on Murphy's payroll.

"You've been digging too deep."

"What's an investor to do?" It was a rhetorical question. "O'Neal's pitch didn't fully satisfy me, so I did some digging. It's called due diligence."

"You did your digging with other investors, then went to Richmond," noted George. "Murphy didn't cotton to that."

I laughed sardonically. "More like folks in New York didn't cotton to it."

"You're still a Texas Ranger, ain't you," stated George. He was fishing.

"Talk like that could put a man six feet under," I advised. "In your case, we might make it seven." The fact that he suggested my ties with the Rangers meant that Murphy suspected something.

George made a searching gaze into my eyes. "Murphy sent that photograph to your wife."

I offered a cool smile. "You think I was born yesterday? I told her to expect it one of these days." Murphy's idiocy was being confirmed right here behind the Union Depot Hotel.

"You think like a lawman," said the big man.

"Well, I run a large ranch. I'm a businessman first. I spent three years with the Texas Rangers, and my dad was a Ranger before me, so I pretty much know how lawmen think. It shouldn't surprise Murphy or you that I just might have some smarts rolling around in this brain."

It appeared that George had run out of questions.

"You run your tail back to Murphy and tell him to back off. Tell him that you're satisfied that I'm not the law. You got that?" I bored into him with a tough gaze.

George nodded, turned, and walked off.

I breathed a sigh of relief and headed for the front desk. I rang the bell to summon the clerk. Given the past twenty-four hours, I believed it made good sense to have him precede me to my room. He wasn't exactly happy about it, but a dollar eased his concerns.

I reckoned that it was time to catch up with Colin O'Neal. I felt as though he represented the final piece of the puzzle toward sewing up the case. Was he still galivanting around Texas cities, luring monied people into investment in the Dallas Oil Company? I didn't especially feature trying to track him down. Neither did I figure this information was within the purview of the hotel desk clerk. Then, it struck me: Mrs. Haskell.

I resolved to pay Mr. and Mrs. Haskell a visit next morning.

As I lay back enjoying the soft luxury of a hotel bed, it came to me that I had to get word to Deputy US Marshal Miller and to Captain Hughes. In addition to updating them on my progress, I hoped to get them to cover my backside. Having survived two bushwhacking attempts and the Aimes assault, I was just a tad concerned as to how long my luck might run. Odds were that one of Murphy's hired guns would eventually get me. This led me to wonder at what had become of my nemesis Kyle McClintock? It had been a blessing that the fool couldn't hit the broadside of a barn with a shotgun at close range, but eventually, he just might get lucky.

I heard an envelope slide under the door. Sighing at having to yield to my natural curiosity and pull my tired bones from the comfort of the bed, I got up and fetched the envelope. I opened it to find a note from Miller. He claimed to have a man tailing me to watch my backside. He didn't apologize for his man missing the bushwhackers or Aimes or George. I didn't have to be a mental giant to figure that Miller's *man* wasn't worth a plug nickel. On the plus side, Miller provided the location of a drop for me to leave any messages. It was about time, especially as I had plenty to relate.

I sighed, climbed back into bed, and fell asleep.

FIFTEEN
THE PLOT THICKENS

TO MY SURPRISE, Mrs. Haskell greeted me. Her husband stood behind, and I couldn't miss the Winchester leaning handily at the side table beside him. "Why, Mr. Dunn. What a pleasant surprise. Do come in." There was relief in her voice, yet I sensed her husband's tension. The two were under considerable stress.

I'd left a note at the drop location that morning after leaving the hotel. The drop was behind some boards at the nearby livery stable. I tried not to say anything in my note that might be connected directly to me while explaining that investors were being cheated and that the Richmond oil field was a sham. I didn't mention the three attempts on my life nor the ledgers that I planned to obtain from Carson this very evening.

The Haskells led me into the library, and Mrs. Haskell proceeded to ask the maid to brew some coffee. "Please have a seat, Mr. Dunn," invited Mr. Haskell. "You can call me Chet. My wife is Matilda."

I figured that the casual tone meant that they'd be quite

forthcoming. "Well, since we're being informal, y'all can call me Luke."

"The Dallas Oil Company is demanding more investment," opened Mrs. Haskell.

"To drive home their demand, they caused a one-week delay in shipment of my cotton. It surely got my attention." Haskell looked at me curiously. "I deal with a lot of folks in my businesses, Luke. I usually get a handle on intentions and character right quick. I know that you own a sizable spread down near Corpus Christi, but my gut says you haven't separated from the Texas Rangers as rumors would have it. I'm right, aren't I?"

"What you don't know isn't likely to get you killed, Chet. I'm afraid I can't give you a straight answer, and that's as far as I'll go."

Matilda Haskell gave her husband one of those *I told you so* looks and poured us all some coffee.

"I did chat with other investors, and they have stories similar to your own. I also went to Richmond. Be assured, there's no drilling. Just some oil derricks lying on their sides and rotting in the Texas sun." I paused for a sip of coffee.

"Colin O'Neal's boss, Gordon Murphy, doesn't especially appreciate my nosing around. There have been three failed attempts on my life in the past couple of days. Let's just say that I've been a very lucky man to still be above the snakes."

Chet Haskell shook his head. His wife was horrified.

"Do you know who these characters work for?" I asked.

They shook their heads tentatively as though fearful of what I was about to share.

"There's a crime-infested organization in New York City loosely called the Irish Mob. They work for a rascally bunch of lawbreakers back in Ireland. Murphy's job is to establish a foothold in Texas. They originally sought to do that by buying into railroads, but then realized the opportunity in oil."

"How do you know this?" asked Mrs. Haskell.

"I did what folks call due diligence. It nearly cost me my life, and it surely would have risked yours, Chet. Once folk like Murphy have you hooked, they'll bleed you dry and cast you aside. I'm sure Murphy wouldn't mind adding cattle and cotton to his fledgling empire." I'd said a mouthful and then some.

The Haskells sat in silence. They were properly embarrassed at the scam they'd fallen for. Mr. Haskell had no idea that his cattle and cotton businesses would be put in peril by having given his wife the opportunity to join the world of business investment. Her naivete had cost them, and they faced the prospect of it costing them plenty more.

The plot had thickened with Murphy going back to the original investors to extort more money. I wished I could tell them about Carson's ledgers. I gave Mrs. Haskell a sympathetic look. "I need to catch up with Colin O'Neal. Do you have any idea where he might be making his pitches?"

"I heard from Bert Falwell that O'Neal was seen eating the other day at the Union Depot Hotel."

Apparently, this had happened while I was down in Richmond. "Do you have any way of finding out whether he's still in town? I'm not quite ready to confront Gordon Murphy."

"I can assure you that he's in town," said Mr. Haskell. "He'll be paying us a visit this evening."

"Y'all agree to most any additional investment that he wants," I advised. "You'll have to trust that I know what I'm doing." I reckoned that O'Neal and I would have a meeting on the trail after his dinner at the Haskell spread.

They nodded, and we finished our coffee. Mr. Haskell explained his far-flung business operations. I reckoned I could learn a thing or two from the man and committed to doing that once this case was resolved.

Carson was good to his word. I found a satchel buried under leaves beneath the live oak. Inside were four ledgers. A quick inspection revealed that the banker had been diligent in tracking the monies of the Irish Mob and the Dallas Oil Company. I had already picked a spot to hide the evidence. I'd be the only person to know the location, though I sent an encrypted message to Captain Hughes, so there were actually two folks who knew.

I ate a fine dinner at the hotel. The sun was casting a golden glow on the western horizon, as I walked to the livery to saddle up and head out toward the Haskell spread to intercept O'Neal. I hadn't gone but a few steps, when there was a massive explosion behind me. Pieces of the Dallas Trust were sent hundreds of feet into the air, and what remained caught fire! It caused my ears to ring for a moment.

Worse! I saw Ernest Carson stagger from the bank and drop to his knees. His screams filled the air as he was fully engulfed in flames. Regrettably, I could do nothing for the man and dared not go near the flames. I'd never seen any human burn to death. It was a horrifying sight to behold.

I saw a shadow of a man running from the conflagration but couldn't make him out in the dark. I figured it was likely one of Murphy's henchmen. As he gained the funds from investors, he was hiring hardened and down-on-their-luck men from Dallas and beyond to better reach out with tentacles of violence. However, I was breathing down Murphy's neck, and I suspected he knew it.

While I was grateful that I possessed the ledgers, I'd have preferred Carson alive to bear witness against the Irish Mob. Hopefully, he'd provided for his family.

It occurred to me that any paper money held in the bank would be consumed by the flames unless the bank vault was fireproof. Hopefully, investor funds were unscathed.

Folks finally came running and attempted a bucket brigade while awaiting the arrival of the fire wagon with its new pump apparatus. It would be a futile effort as the building was fully consumed.

The stable boy passed me on the run to join the bucket brigade. I left the chaos behind and resumed my walk to the livery. I left a couple of dollars with a note and took the same cayuse I'd used previously. Saddled up, I headed toward the Haskell ranch.

The moon still hung full in the night sky, so I took extra care in concealing myself. Ironically, I chose the same spot that Aimes and Murphy's muscle man George had intercepted me a few days back.

Patience is counted among the seven cardinal virtues. I recalled Deputy US Marshal Bass Reeves advising me that it was one of the very most important qualities necessary for a successful lawman. I'd say that it was among the very toughest. I dearly wanted to get my hands on O'Neal but would be constrained by the heavenly virtues of prudence, justice, temperance, and fortitude. Such constraints didn't exactly make my life as a lawman easy. Being undercover simply added to my present challenges.

As I waited for O'Neal, I thought of Gordon Murphy.

The man was suspicious of me enough that he'd decided to not take any chances. By now, he was extremely frustrated that his hired killers had repeatedly failed him. Even George, his ox of a muscle man, had failed him. It wouldn't be long before I'd be confronting Murphy. Ideally, I'd be wearing the Texas Ranger badge and putting the man in handcuffs. This led me to think beyond wrapping up this case. I'd promised Cassie that I'd hang up the badge for good. The very idea ran counter to my father's lawman blood that ran through my veins. Hopefully, I'd still be around to face my promise.

O'Neal was taking his sweet time with the Haskells. Chet Haskell was a strong businessman, but the Irish Mob had him by his *cajones*. If he pushed too hard, they'd destroy his cotton trade and then keep his beeves from market. Matilda Haskell had naively embroiled them in an extortion racket that exacted big money. Hopefully, I'd be able to salvage some portion of their operations by bringing Murphy to justice.

The sound of hooves on the hard-packed rocky road soon awakened me from my musings. My patience was to be put aside at last. In the silvery moonlight, I couldn't miss Colin O'Neal's slim form jouncing along on a nondescript gelding. He wasn't a natural horseman.

I urged my horse from behind the trees. "Colin O'Neal!" I called out.

Much to my surprise, a startled O'Neal put his heels to his cayuse's ribs and took off. But a hundred feet later, he was hugging a cactus.

I rode easily over to him. He was a sight to behold; certainly not the well-dressed slick pitchman selling investments in the Dallas Oil Company. I dismounted and offered him a hand.

"Y-y-you sonofabitch," he said through teeth clenched in

pain even as he stood with my help. There's nothing like cactus spines to rattle a man to his very soul. His eyes came into focus and widened, as he recognized me. "You!" he bellowed.

"You got that right, O'Neal. It was me last time I checked." I laid my steely-eyed look on him. "We're going to have a little chat."

"But Murphy…" his words trailed off.

"Yes. He keeps trying to have me killed. Looks like it hasn't worked out for him yet."

My attempt at sarcasm didn't resonate especially well with O'Neal. The man began to grasp the vulnerability of his present situation. "What do yuh be wanting with me?" He inadvertently lapsed into an Irish brogue that he normally disguised.

"Now, what sort of question is that, Colin? You don't mind me calling you Colin, do you?" I stifled an ironic smile. "You sure know how to sweet-talk folks into parting with their money. You're even quite good at hiding that Irish accent of yours and burying it under our fine Texas twang." I gave him a gaze aimed at penetrating deep into the very depths of his evil soul. "You hook them, grab their money, and then bleed them dry. Do I have that right?"

"Who do yuh be?"

"I'm just an investor who likes to know what I'm investing in." I tried to offer up a sincere smile. "Your boss man seems to have taken a dislike to me."

O'Neal nodded. "Yuh be right 'bout that," he observed resignedly. He winced as he began to pluck a cactus spine or two from his hands.

"So, I'm correct about your role in this?"

"Murphy's goin' to head back to New York. I will lead Texas operations." O'Neal's Texas twang began to reemerge.

I couldn't help but laugh as I looked at the disheveled mess standing before me. O'Neal was a caricature of evil, but now stood covered in the dust and cactus spines. Was this slimy critter destined to lead a crime operation? "Did you have anything to do with blowing up the Dallas Trust?" The question had lingered on my mind ever since I observed Ernest Carson's grisly death.

"They blew it up?" he exclaimed.

"Ernest Carson burned to death," I said.

"Nasty way to go," observed O'Neal. "Guess some call it collateral damage."

"Did Murphy order it?" I persisted.

"Can't be saying," responded O'Neal.

"Can't you now?" I said, as I drew my Bowie knife from its sheath behind my back. Its razor-sharp tip quickly found its way beside O'Neal's neck. "Don't dare move a muscle, Colin. Now, you be straight with me. Did Gordon Murphy order the bank to be blown and Carson killed?"

"You some sort of lawman or something?" said the Irishman, as he winced from a cactus spine and felt the prick of my knife at his throat. His was awakening to his situation being a tad vulnerable.

"Used to be. Now, I'm a concerned investor in Dallas Oil Company. Answer my question," I insisted. I patted him down and relieved him of a dainty little pocket pistol and a knife. I looked down just enough to see that he'd peed his pants.

A trickle of blood appeared at O'Neal's neck at the tip of my knife. He swallowed hard and sweat began to form on his forehead. "He might have," said O'Neal.

I pressed my knife harder. More blood. More sweat.

"Y-y-yes. Murphy ordered it."

I pulled back the knife a little. "Well, that was easy enough, wasn't it?" I paused to let that register in his evil mind. "You will deliver a message from me to Gordon Murphy. Do I make myself clear?"

The man nodded vigorously.

"Good. I want you to set up a meeting between me and Murphy in the back room at the Union Depot Hotel tomorrow evening at seven. Repeat that back to me."

O'Neal shuffled his dirty boots like a school kid being punished. "Meet Mr. Murphy tomorrow night at seven. Back room. Union Depot Hotel," he mumbled.

"Good. Now, you wait here and I'll fetch your horse. It's a long walk back to town." I mounted up and rode down the road to O'Neal's mount. The poor gelding gave me a reluctant look but let me lead the poor beast back to O'Neal.

By now, Murphy's henchman had removed the most irritating of the cactus spines. He'd been fortunate to have not hit the cactus butt first. O'Neal climbed gingerly into the saddle, gave me a nasty look, and rode off.

I wished I were a fly on the wall to listen to him relate this evening's encounter to Murphy. I had woven my web. Now, I had to make like a spider and trap my prey. First, getting messages to Miller and Hughes were critically important. I didn't feature tomorrow evening's meeting without backup.

Missing my Cassie weighed ever heavier on my mind. I vowed to avoid extended cases in the future. It wasn't fair to her or me. I knew my dad was often gone for weeks, and somehow my mom endured. I'd had enough of it. It was looking more and more like I'd be true to my promise to quit.

SIXTEEN
TEXAS RANGER AGAIN

I PLACED notes in the drop with the time and place of the meeting with Murphy. I doubted that Hughes could respond in any sort of timely fashion, given his being in Corpus Christi, but he could alert Texas Rangers up here in Dallas. Deputy US Marshal Miller, on the other hand, was close at hand. There was no excuse for his not joining the party.

I spent the next morning reviewing the bank ledger books in greater detail. From what limited knowledge I had of accounting, unraveling Carson's entries and notes took several hours. I had enough to arrest Murphy and O'Neal, but it would be up to the government to put the case together in detail. While some of the braver investors were willing to testify, including the Haskells, the hard evidence of the ledgers was the key to my case.

I took a warm bath, shaved, and donned a clean shirt. The rest of my attire was sort of clean. I wore the jacket so as to hide my shoulder holster with the Smith & Wesson nestled inside. Of course, I checked to be sure it was loaded. I took my Texas Ranger badge from a secret compartment in my satchel. I tried to envision the look on Gordon Murphy's face when his suspicions of me were confirmed. I lacked handcuffs, but reckoned Miller or one of the Rangers would be so equipped. I buffed the badge and pinned it to my shirt. I glanced at my image in the mirror. I felt pretty damned good.

It was getting toward five o'clock, so I removed the badge and headed to dinner. I reckoned I'd be early enough to avoid any accidental meetup with any of the Irish Mob. Actually, I thought of them as the Black Gold Mob. It had a nice ring to it. I figured it was catchy enough that the newspapers would surely pick up on it.

I seated myself in the dining room and ordered a steak. I was feeling that I was deserving of a good steak dinner. As I was finishing up and enjoying a few last sips of coffee, imagine my surprise when Kyle McClintock strolled in.

He took a furtive look my way and exited right quickly.

It left me wondering whether Murphy might be planning some shenanigans. It was all the more reason for my backup to show up. I headed back to my room.

As I reached the head of the stairs, I peered cautiously down the dimly lit hallway toward my room. I wasn't up to being greeted by another shotgun blast. However, there was someone standing at the door to my room. What was Lilly doing here? First McClintock and now Lilly. It was like some sort of reunion.

"Lilly? What are you doing here?" I asked.

"I come to warn you. Murphy is going to kill you."

"Here in the hotel?" I pressed.

She was shaking like a leaf. "Yes," she replied.

I opened the door and invited her into my room. "Where did you hear this?"

"George told me. He said that I should warn you."

I suppose that George must have found some respect for

me after our most recent encounter. He likely was unable to warn me himself. Little wonder that McClintock had shown up. What other hired guns awaited me in the back room of the Union Depot Hotel? Would tonight's steak dinner have been my final meal? How naïve to think Murphy could be trusted. I had to keep reminding myself that his Black Gold Mob held no scruples. "You've done the right thing, Lilly."

Tears welled up as she buried her face in my chest. "I don't want you to die, Mr. Dunn."

I gently held her at arm's length. "I'll be all right. You stay here. I'll come back here after the meeting with Murphy."

"You're going through with it?" She was shocked at what I was saying. She wiped her tears.

I drew my Texas Ranger badge from my pocket and pinned it on.

Now, Lilly's tears turned to a laugh. "You're a Texas Ranger!" she said with surprise. Then she cocked her head with a winsome smile. "Does the badge make you bullet-proof?" she chided.

"As I understand it, one riot, one Ranger," I retorted. "I reckon to handle Murphy's bunch." The clock on the dresser chimed seven o'clock. The time had come.

"You're going?" she repeated in a tone of disbelief.

"I'll be back." With that, I exited the room. I wish I were as self-assured as I'd tried to sound with Lilly. It appeared that I'd be facing an ambush to top all ambushes. They'd find enough lead in me to plant me permanently at the bottom of the Brazos River. I wasn't normally much of a praying man, but I sure was praying that the note I sent about backup had reached Marshal Miller and Captain Hughes. On that note, this was the sort of situation in which a man became acquainted with his Maker.

I closed my hotel room door behind me, hitched up my pants, and took a deep breath. Once again, I checked the loads in my gun. Six bullets. I hoped I wouldn't need more. I felt as though I might be about to fight a roaring fire with a tin cup full of water. I strode up the hallway and headed down the stairs. Time seemed to stand still. I thought about Cassie and prayed that I'd see her and my children again.

At last, I found myself facing the door of the hotel's back room. I heard Murphy inside, barking orders to what I figured to be at least three others.

"Put your damned gun away! Don't want him seeing guns first thing!" demanded Murphy from within the room.

I shook my head. Who was he kidding? I could just about smell their guns through the hotel walls. I knocked on the door. The silence in the room could be cut like warm butter with a dull knife.

The door opened ever-so-slowly. Unsurprisingly, George greeted me. "Let's have your gun," he requested. As the words left his mouth, he caught sight of my Texas Ranger badge. The expression that painted itself across his face was of total resignation to his fate.

What an incredibly hollow request! If they thought I was that stupid, then what I did next forever dissuaded them of that. "Sorry, George," I said, as I wrapped one arm around his prodigious neck and filled my free hand with the Smith & Wesson. Its muzzle pressed deep into George's back. "Y'all are under arrest. Place your hardware on the table, gentlemen."

A mix of surprise and anger contorted Murphy's face. "You damned traitor!" he hissed. O'Neal and the gunman beside him drew their revolvers and opened fire. Muzzle flashes and smoke filled my field of vision. I felt George's thick body stop round after round. It was all I could do to support his literally dead weight as he sagged against me. George made for a great shield, as he must have absorbed nearly a dozen bullets. The room was now thick with gun smoke, but I took my time and was able to make out my shadowy targets. I aimed carefully and pulled my trigger once...twice. O'Neal and the gunmen each fell mortally wounded. Murphy was nowhere to be seen. Where had the sonofabitch disappeared to?

I let George slump to the floor.

O'Neal fired one more shot. The bullet nicked my ear. I heard his gun click on empty. With that, I strode to a curtain along the far wall of the room. An open window revealed Murphy's escape route. "Damn!" I cursed to myself.

Noises behind me announced the arrival of Marshal Miller and three Texas Rangers.

"Don't just stand there!" I hollered. "He's getting away!"

Miller laughed. "Afraid not, Ranger Dunn!" he boomed. He nodded toward the door, where lots of angry yelling in the hallway announced that Murphy hadn't gotten very far. A moment later, the Irish mobster was dragged into the room by two marshals.

"Glad y'all finally got here," I chided the marshal.

Miller passed the handcuffs to me. "How about you do the honors, Ranger Dunn."

"Yuh damned traitor to yer race!" screamed Murphy, as I wrangled his arms behind his back and cuffed him. I turned his wrists extra hard, eliciting a painful groan. I'd have done worse to him, if the law permitted.

I placed my mouth inches from his ear. "You're lucky not to have eaten my lead, Murphy," I snarled at him. "I expect that your friends back in New York City are going to be none too happy with another of your failures. You going to enjoy the walls of the Huntsville Unit for a few years before your Irish Mob can exact punishment." The prison in Huntsville was nicknamed the Walls Unit and had harbored the worst of the worst lawbreakers in Texas. There was a fair chance that Murphy would never get free of it alive.

Marshal Miller stepped up. "You did a hell of a job, Dunn," said Miller admiringly. "Thanks to you, we have those ledgers in federal custody."

Federal custody, I thought. I reckoned to let the state and federal folks fight this one out. "Pleased to have been of service, Marshal. I'll get you a written report and then be on my way home."

I planned to call Cassie, relax for a day, and then head home. First, I felt a duty to relieve Lilly's concerns. I headed to my room. I was relieved, yet something lingered in my lawman mind, as though there were still loose ends.

For some reason, I paused at the door. That gave me a moment to hear a muffled noise inside as though someone was trying to call out through a gag over their mouth. I stood aside and replaced the two spent shells in my revolver.

I knocked.

One, two, three, four, five bullets blasted through the center panel of the door.

I made a sound as though I'd fallen and added a seriously realistic mortally wounded groan. I heard Lilly scream as the shooter's footsteps pounded toward the door.

The gunman confidently swung it open and found himself looking down at the menacing muzzle of my Smith & Wesson planted in his belly. He raised his gun, but paused.

"Well, partner, did you fire five shots or six?" I challenged. "Can you pull the trigger before your guts are spread all over the room?"

His eyes grew wide. Sweat beaded on his forehead. "Damn," he uttered. He dropped the gun and raised his hands.

I glanced inside to be sure Lilly was all right, then heard footsteps behind me. A couple of Miller's deputies had responded at the sounds of the gunshots. I smiled. "Good to see you fellows. You can add this one to your collection." I shook my head forbearingly. Once again, my backup had arrived after the threat had ended. As he was being handcuffed, I picked up the gunman's weapon. "Lookee here! You did have one round left," I called out and handed the gun to the deputy.

I stood for a moment watching the gunman being dragged away. It left me wondering what sort of residual threats still remained from Murphy's operation.

"Mr. Dunn?" asked a trembling Lilly.

I'd nearly forgotten her in the melee. "Everything's okay, Lilly." Once again, she buried herself in my arms.

"How?" she asked.

"Like I said, one riot, one Ranger." I laughed at the underlying irony in my assurance. I'd been lucky. And I'd just been lucky again. Luck has a way of running out, and I was pretty-much done pitting my intuition and experience against plain old dumb luck. I held Lilly at arm's length. Her good intentions and concerns for me outweighed the immoral poisons of her chosen profession. "You are a good woman, Lilly. Too good for this sort of life. Don't go back to the Iron Front Saloon. If you make your way down to Corpus Christi, I know some folks who would be pleased to take you in and give you some work you can be proud of. You might even meet a real man."

"Do you truly believe that, Mr. Dunn?" she asked hopefully.

"That's Texas Ranger Dunn to you, young lady." I gave a broad grin. "The future is up to you. I'd be pleased to help." I thought back on how my dad had helped a prostitute named Scarlet turn away from her past to begin a legitimate haberdashery business in Corpus Christi. Scarlet would be pleased to help Lilly.

Lilly's crystal blue eyes locked onto my sincerity. "I will do that, Mr.…er…Texas Ranger Dunn."

"Now, you be on your way. I'll be heading home tomorrow."

As she gathered her things, I got to thinking that I hadn't heard hide nor hair of Kyle McClintock. What might he be up to? I was thinking on that, when Lilly kissed my cheek and twirled her way up the hotel hallway.

I put my hand to the spot she'd kissed. Maybe, she would get her life together.

SEVENTEEN
MCCLINTOCK PART TWO

COME MORNING, I headed to the train depot. I'd be riding south today toward home. Murphy and his Black Gold Mob were finished. The vault at Dallas Trust had withstood the explosion and flames, so investors would recover some of their losses. Likewise, the state would recover most of the money I'd used in entrapping Murphy's operation. Here's where I preferred the story to end. Ha!

Unanswered questions still lingered. Where was Kyle McClintock? I'd thought he might have been one of Murphy's gunmen in that back-room ambush at the hotel. Why wasn't he there? No *cajones*?

As I sat in the passenger car, tuning out the conversations surrounding me, I tried to put myself inside Murphy's perverted mind. What might he do to make my life miserable? Cassie! Murphy's ace-in-the-hole, so to speak, was to hurt Cassie to get back at me. Who better to send on that assignment than McClintock, with his built-in jealousy and hatred of me?

Now, I found myself incredibly anxious and frustrated. I couldn't get to Heaven's Gate Ranch fast enough. Was

McClintock already there and wreaking his mayhem? As the train steamed into the Corsicana depot, I leaped off and ran to the engineer. I flashed my Texas Ranger badge and told him to hold the train while I sent an emergency telegram. I reached out to Sheriff McTiernan and to Captain Hughes. As I turned to return to the train, I reversed myself.

"I need to use your telephone," I said to the agent.

"Excuse me," he said, hesitating with his hand on the receiver.

I wrestled it free and placed a call to Cassie. I was relieved that she answered.

"Lucas?" she asked.

"You're in danger. McClintock is coming after you. Get Red John and Nick. I'm on my way home." I hung up before she could respond.

The train engineer was exceedingly impatient, and the passengers none too happy. I didn't give a damn. I waved the engineer to pull out and climbed back onboard. I flashed my badge at the angry passengers, and that seemed to mostly settle them down. I plopped down in my seat. This train simply couldn't get to Corpus Christi fast enough.

It was after dark when the train screeched and hissed its way into the Corpus Christi station. I was still getting annoyed looks from passengers. Of course, they hadn't a clue as to what was going on, and no one had asked me to explain. Ignoring them, I grabbed my satchel and disembarked as quickly as my legs would carry me. I approached McTiernan's office and the jail on my way to the livery. The place was dark. I knocked on the door, but there was no answer. He was likely either asleep at home or had ridden out to my place to investigate any threat. I prayed that it was the latter.

I jogged to the livery stable, as though a hundred feet or so at a faster pace would make all that much difference. I checked the stalls and finally found my stallion with the Heaven's Gate brand. I had no idea what I owed for his keep, but I'd worry about that later. I fetched my saddle and tack hanging on the nearby wall and was soon heading toward home. I wished that I'd brought my Winchester, but I'd have to deal with that as best as I could.

The moon was still throwing a lot of light on the landscape, and I was familiar with the road, so I set as fast a pace as I reckoned my cayuse could handle. It took me until dawn to cover the better than twenty miles to Heaven's Gate.

By the time the purplish gold of the rising sun had begun to appear behind me, I'd worked out a strategy to approach a likely threatening situation. Instead of riding up the lane from the gateway arch to the house, I circled far around to the south. I was all ears but heard nothing. Reaching the creek that I was intimately familiar with from my growing up here, I tethered my horse and started up the creek toward the old swimming hole. From there, I snuck up the steep path toward the big house, bunkhouse, and barn. This was the path my mom had used years before to do laundry at the creek and had climbed it the day she fought the Comanche that killed her folks. The top of the incline offered a clear view of the ranch buildings. I kept my head low and peered around.

There were no stirrings other than a few chickens and a rooster that appeared ready to announce the sunrise. Had I misjudged? Had McClintock not yet arrived? Or had he already wreaked his evil and lay out there somewhere to bushwhack me?

Upon reflection, I decided to stay put and see what came to life beside the chickens. I didn't have long to wait. Brody and Tess came trotting out, noses to the ground as they investigated for anything that might have passed in the night. They hadn't discovered me just yet, but they would soon enough. Where were Cassie and the boys? Where were my cousins Red John and Nick? What about Sheriff McTiernan? Had any Texas Rangers shown up? Unanswered questions swirled through my head.

The answer finally came from the direction of my folks' house behind me and to the west. Gunshots! My gut feel told me that Cassie had moved there after my warning. She rightly figured that it was a bit more easily defended than our house. The shooting was sporadic; just enough to be pinning someone down.

Seizing the opportunity, I headed for the house. I reckoned to grab my Winchester carbine. Upon entering, it appeared obvious that Cassie and the boys had left in a hurry. There were no signs of any struggle.

With my carbine in hand and pockets filled with ammunition, I headed for the barn. Horses were in their stalls. Tornado whinnied a greeting at me. "Later, boy, we'll take a long ride later," I assured the big stallion. Everything in the barn was in order except the stalls needed mucking.

I decided it was best to walk to what sounded like the scene of a small battle. My folks had built the house after assuming control of the vast ranch holdings of Edward Thorpe. It was only four miles away, so I reckoned to get there in about an hour at a fast walk. It occurred to me that I was starving. Not knowing what lay ahead, I went back into the house and retrieved some venison jerky and a canteen of water.

The uncertainty of what lay ahead was concerning. Was a lone gunman, perhaps Kyle McClintock, keeping a houseful of Dunns at bay?

The house finally came into view. It was deathly silent. Two saddled horses were hitched to the post out front. There was no further gunfire.

"McClintock! You there?" I shouted.

No response.

"McClintock?" I yelled the name again. The sound of hooves trailing off to the north came to my ears. Had the cowardly bushwhacker run off?

I walked the last few yards toward the house. "Cassie?" I called out.

There was a long silence, then the front door creaked open. Cassie stepped out with my dad's Winchester in hand. "Luke? Luke, you're safe!" she called.

"He looks to be gone," I said.

Cassie left the house and ran into my arms, burying her face in my chest. "It was horrible, Lucas," she whispered. "Sean and Bode were scared half to death."

"Was it McClintock?" I asked.

She nodded. "I headed here after your call. McClintock arrived soon after I'd run out. I could hear him firing his guns in frustration. He came here, and your mom and I stood him off."

"What about Red John or Nick? How about the sheriff?"

"Guess they never got the word. Red John and Nick were pretty regular about checking on me. They wouldn't have missed this if they'd known. Our ranch hands Pedro and Jimmy were buying supplies down in Falfurrias. It was just us, Lucas."

"I'm proud of you for holding the coward off, sweetheart." I looked off in the direction by which McClintock had escaped. "Kyle must have seen me coming and figured the odds weren't in his favor. I'll bet he doesn't yet know that Gordon Murphy and his Irish Mob are no more."

"What are we going to do, Lucas?" Cassie still clung to me.

"Raising a posse is a possibility, but McClintock's trail is hot. We must eliminate him from our worries."

"You're going after him?"

I nodded. Cassie was in my arms, and I didn't want to release my hold.

"He might be setting an ambush this very minute," Cassie warned.

"I've tracked down better men than he. I must go after him." I really had no choice. Importantly. McClintock was on land that I knew like the back of my hand. If I gave him too much time, he'd lead me into territory I was less familiar with. "I must," I repeated.

By this time, my mom, Sean, and Bode had emerged from the house. The boys came running. Brody and Tess had even tracked me from the house. There I stood in the midst of a dust-raising gathering of loved ones. I was torn, but duty called. Actually, this was far more than about duty. This was about protecting my family.

"Let's get back to our home, Cassie. I have to saddle up Tornado while you put together some trail supplies. This might take a day or two." Dang, but I sure sounded confident. I guess this was the confidence of a lawman who'd walked into an ambush at a hotel back room and come out unscathed. Now, I found myself dealing with what amounted to collateral damage from the Black Gold Mob. I suppose I should have counted myself lucky that Murphy had assigned this revenge business to McClintock and not someone more capable.

I thanked my mom for providing comfort to Cassie and a place to fend off McClintock, then gathered my family and headed back to our home.

Tracking McClintock wasn't going to be easy despite the man's failings. The fact that McClintock wasn't a skilled woodsman was challenging for me by virtue of his unpredictability. An experienced hunter understands wildlife and their habits. McClintock's habits, his tendencies, were a mystery. His naivete worked against me.

Cassie was silent as we walked back to the house.

The boys cavorted along the way. They hadn't a care in the world, and I envied that.

Upon entering our home, Cassie turned to face me. "You are still hanging up the badge?"

I went to hug her, but she pulled away.

She stood before me with arms folded and the sort of expression across her beautiful face that no man wants to face.

"I promised," I finally responded. "But I need it to track down McClintock. If I have to kill him, it must be while attempting to arrest him. Without the badge, it'd be murder."

She nodded slowly, then hugged me and headed to gather victuals for the trail.

I advised her to let Red John, Nick, and our hands know what I was up to, as well as Sheriff McTiernan if he came by. Finally, I went upstairs to dress for hunting. I figured to wear buckskins to better blend in with the landscape. We were well into fall now, so leaves were turning and nights growing chillier. I packed gloves in my saddlebags along with extra ammunition, fire starters, and more.

I headed back downstairs and found Cassie packing the last of the jerky and some bear sign in a sack. I watched her for a moment, taking in her beauty before she looked up to see me.

"We don't have time for that, Lucas," she said with a provocative smile that spoke of making up for these lost moments upon my return.

We'd been apart for far too long while I was on these assignments. I was determined to compensate if there was any atonement to be had.

Sean and Bode were perplexed, as they watched me saddle up Tornado. They watched, but not in the carefree, playful way they normally would. Even Brody and Tess were subdued.

My hug with Cassie was a long one. My, but I missed her so. I kissed and hugged the boys, ruffled the dogs, and mounted up. I nudged Tornado forward and didn't look back. I couldn't. Grown men don't cry.

EIGHTEEN
TRACKING A KILLER

I LOOKED for McClintock's trail near the place where I'd heard him riding north from the ranch. It hadn't rained in a week, so any hoofprints had made lasting impressions in the soil. It took me a solid hour, but I finally found tracks that looked to be recent enough.

I followed the tracks for about a mile, then came to a spot where the horse and rider had rested. Examining boot prints, I noticed that the right boot dug deeper into the soil. Then, to my surprise, I found more than tracks. My eagle eyes spotted a drop of dried blood on a rock. McClintock had been wounded. The boot depression suggested that he was limping. Had he taken a bullet from Cassie or my mom? Looking around, I found some scraps of cloth. McClintock had bandaged himself.

Upon leaving, my wounded prey had turned northwest toward the hill country of central Texas. There, he'd find plenty of places to set an ambush. He was surely confident that I'd be following him.

I wondered how he might be fixed for food and ammunition. Setting an ambush was only as good as a man's patience and his empty belly. I smiled, as I mounted up. With several hours head start, McClintock was still at a considerable advantage.

My prey was making no effort to cover his trail. I simply followed at a leisurely pace. My eyes were drawn aloft at a pair of circling buzzards. Had McClintock bled out?

I soon came upon a stand of live oak. Coyotes were working on some carrion. A breeze picked up and carried the odor of human flesh my way. The coyotes were feasting on human carrion, and the buzzards were waiting for them to have their fill. I dismounted to investigate. The dead man wasn't McClintock, but very well could have been his victim. I chased off the coyotes. Tying my bandana over my nose to minimize the terrible odor, I took a closer look at the victim. There was no question that this was a victim. Despite the ravenous coyotes, I could see at least two bullet holes. I rifled the man's pockets and found some identification.

The man's horse stood among the trees a few yards away. I could see that the rifle scabbard was empty, so reckoned that McClintock had increased his firepower. I chuckled ironically at that. It only took one rifle and one bullet to bushwhack someone. Maybe, he expected a posse. Last but not least, I found the dead man's pistol. It had been fired once. Whether he'd hit anything was anybody's guess.

With my prey hours ahead, coyotes yipping and growling at me, and buzzards hungrily circling overhead, I reckoned it was useless to bury the man at this juncture. Besides, any grave would be shallow enough that the critters would have it dug up in no time. I relieved the dead man's horse of its tack and sent it on its way. I rummaged around in the saddlebags, but there was nothing of consequence. McClintock had likely taken anything of value.

I walked back to Tornado and climbed aboard. The encounter here might have delayed McClintock some. But then, I had stopped to investigate, so I likely hadn't closed the gap. "Let's go, boy," I said with a squeeze of my knees into his flanks. Tornado shook his head playfully, and we headed out.

McClintock's life had sure spiraled downward. Aside from his assault on Cassie, he'd committed two murders. I had no idea what he might have done for Murphy, but I had enough to arrest him and likely see him be the main guest at his very own necktie party. I did want to bring him in alive. However, if he tried to bushwhack me, I realized that I might have little choice but to kill him. It would be justice without satisfaction.

I alternately rode and walked Tornado. With no idea as to how far I might be traveling, I had to keep him as fresh as possible. McClintock was making no effort to hide his trail. He wasn't even back trailing to see whether he was being followed. There was no more blood sign, but his horse's hooves left a clear track in the soft soil. I'd been tracking him for two full days. He crossed the Nueces River, and it was on the north bank of the Frio River that I found evidence of an extended rest. He'd had the sense to not make a fire, but I saw the remnants of what was likely the victuals stolen from his most recent victim. While it irked me that the killer had no respect for the land, it paled in comparison to his lack of respect for life.

The path of the man I had known as a teen had taken a deep plunge down the dark side. For whatever reason, he held envy for me. I was bigger, stronger, had a famous lawman father, and, most consequential to McClintock, I won the prettiest girl in South Texas. Above and beyond the evil road the man's life had taken, he held a personal animosity toward me about winning the woman he so desperately sought. Was it worth killing for? He thought so.

I hoped I might catch up to him before he reached the hill country. It appeared that he intended to ride through Sabinal and head up to Concan. Once there, he'd have plenty of places to set an ambush. "What do you think, Tornado? Can we catch him?" A snort and a whinny answered my plea. Tornado picked up his pace before I asked him. I know he'd missed me while I was traipsing around Dallas and Corsicana and was now overjoyed to once again be on the trail with me. Such was the bond between horse and man.

Day four arrived. I sensed that I was closing in on my prey. It figured that Mother Nature was about to step in. Dark clouds were roiling up to the northwest. Rain would obliterate the hoof prints that had been so helpful.

The first hint of the hill country now lay ahead. The trail was rockier, so any trace imprints from horse's hooves mattered ever less in the scheme of things. I'd hunted up here, and it was a day north of here that I'd snuck up on Garth Jones and foiled his planned ambush of me. Could I do the same with McClintock?

The man had to be curious as to who was following him, if anyone. Yet, there was still no sign of his having checked his backtrail. I wondered whether he'd heard about the demise of the Irish Mob operation? At the rate he was traveling, I reckoned as not. It likely wouldn't change the present situation.

With a general idea of where McClintock was headed and my fair knowledge of the countryside, I decided to take a gamble and attempt to sneak around him. By getting ahead, I could get the drop on him.

I turned off his trail and headed Tornado up an incline. At the top, I paused to survey the area. I happened to look down, and there were the familiar tracks of McClintock's cayuse. Well, I'd be hornswoggled, the man finally back-trailed. It was now a fair bet that he'd seen me. Now, the hunt turned very real. He likely figured to set his ambush in a ravine a couple of miles up the trail. Fancying that he was the hunter, he was likely feeling very confident. By now, he might also have become mindful of the fact that he was a poor marksman. He'd want to position himself overlooking the natural trail where he couldn't miss.

It was time to teach the man that I was the hunter, not he. I rode Tornado at a walk just the other side of the ridge-line that McClintock had back-trailed on. There were several stands of trees that could accommodate a bush-whacker. Which one might he choose?

I sensed that the fugitive was close, so I dismounted. I removed my spurs and stuffed them into my saddlebag. I slipped the Winchester carbine from its scabbard and checked the load. I did the same with my trusty Smith & Wesson revolver. I ground-hitched Tornado. I paused and took a bite of venison jerky to relax me, then began my short walk up to the top of the ridge. Three clusters of trees presented themselves below me. This was the sloppiest of ambushes ever concocted. He'd hitched his horse to the cluster to my right. The grouping of trees in the center revealed the backside of none other than Kyle McClintock. Dang, but I could even make out his butt crack, as he squatted with rifle ready. He was a mere twenty feet from the trail, so he would have easily bushwhacked me.

I eased my way down the grassy slope as silently as possible. The last thing a hunter wants to do is spook his prey. I reckoned that about fifty feet away would be a good position to announce myself. The distance would also challenge McClintock's marksmanship.

I was in position. McClintock was intently watching the trail. I decided to let my Winchester do the announcing. I levered a round into the receiver. McClintock's hackles went up. He knew he'd been caught. "Drop the rifle and raise your hands, Kyle," I said evenly and with authority.

It was plain that McClintock's mind was racing as to what to do. He had to know that I'd take him back to face the hangman.

"Don't do it, Kyle. You're under arrest. Don't make it any tougher than it need be."

He still hadn't moved. "You always fancied yourself superior to everybody, Dunn."

"Drop the gun and raise your hands," I repeated. "Don't be foolish."

I saw him take a deep breath. It was a natural signal that he was about to take action. He stood, spun, aimed, and took my bullet square in the center of his chest. His rifle dropped, as he clutched at the wound. His eyes looked pleadingly at me. "Yuh done killed me," he gasped and fell on his face. It was an utterly inglorious end to a bitter man.

I walked over and tossed his rifle aside. Turning him onto his back, I relieved him of his revolver. He gasped for air, but my bullet had pretty much destroyed his lungs. He weakly motioned me to come close. I leaned in. "Y...yer the better man." They were Kyle McClintock's final words.

I fetched McClintock's horse, wrapped the body in his blanket, and tied the dead man's body across his saddle. I didn't feature traveling the four days back home with a dead body in tow, so I decided to head to Uvalde and hitch a ride on the Southern Pacific. While on board the train, I'd write a report and send it to Captain Hughes with a copy to Deputy US Marshal Miller as a courtesy. After all, it was what I reckoned to be the last piece of the Black Gold Mob case.

The stationmaster was none too pleased about freighting a dead body. I had to have a makeshift coffin hammered together and securely nailed shut. With McClintock's body in a freight car, Tornado riding with the livestock, and me enjoying the creature comforts of a modern Southern Pacific Railroad passenger car, all coupled with one transfer in San Antonio, we'd arrive in Corpus Christi none the worse for wear.

McClintock's makeshift coffin was loaded onto a borrowed wagon at the Corpus Christi depot. I was quite pleased to deliver it to Sheriff McTiernan, though I wasn't convinced that he shared in my joy of being rid of McClintock and all he represented to me and my family.

I sent off my reports to Miller and Hughes, figuring to call Captain Hughes in a day or so.

As I pointed Tornado toward home, he seemed to know that the hunt was over. His little horse brain was likely already filled with dreams of the mares back at Heaven's Gate Ranch. What could I say? I sure was missing my own sweetheart. This last leg of my trip home couldn't pass by soon enough.

The sun was kissing the western hills, as I rode up to the house. I figured to raise a bit of a homecoming ruckus, so fired a single shot into the air.

It took but a moment for the front door to swing open and Cassie to emerge with carbine in hand. "Lucas!" she hollered. The rifle went skittering along the gallery. I barely had a chance to slide from my saddle as she just about flew into my arms. A long kiss sealed my welcome.

"Did you?"

"He'll never bother us again," I assured her.

"Let's get Tornado to the barn," she said, grabbing his bridle and pulling me along by my arm. "The hands are off to Nuecestown and kids are asleep."

In but minutes, we were rolling half-naked in barn hay. We'd itch later, but that didn't matter for now. My, but it was wonderful to fully immerse myself in passions with my wife.

Soon, we lay back exhausted in the hay. I did grab a horse blanket to ward off the chill of the night air. "I love you, Cassie Dunn," I said as I reached into the pocket of my jacket lying in a heap alongside us. I placed my Texas Ranger badge on her bare belly.

"Ooooh, that's cold!" She picked it up and held it above us, allowing the sun to dance off the polished silver. Cassie turned to me. "I love you, too, Lucas." She looked lovingly into my eyes. "If you ever feel called…" She let the words hang.

I'd delivered on my promise, but she was giving me the freedom to return to the Rangers if I so chose. This is what true love was about. Cassie knew that the blood of a lawman still ran in my veins. My dad had it, her grandfather had it. She's settled it in her heart.

I waited a couple of days before calling Captain Hughes. He was still with the Frontier Battalion patrolling the Rio

Grande. By dumb luck, I caught him at the office in Harlingen.

"Captain?" I greeted.

"Why, Mr. Dunn, looks like you wrapped up the Irish Mob," he opened sort of matter-of-factly. "You quittin' me again?"

I responded with a prolonged silence.

"Well?" he pressed.

"I'm fixing to spend time with my family, Captain."

"You promised your wife, didn't you?"

"Yes, sir. But Cassie says I'm free to take up the badge."

"You married a good woman, Texas Ranger Dunn," observed Hughes.

"Thanks, Captain. I sure enough agree with you on that."

"Things are stirring up south of the Rio Grande. President Diaz is a bit besieged by his opponents. Not much happening just yet, but you know these Mexicans are a passionate people. We're making sure trouble doesn't spill north of the border."

"Sounds like there's a bit to be concerned about, Captain."

"Well, Luke, you tend to your family. If trouble gets past us and spills into your neck of the woods, you are clear to pin that badge back on your chest. No swearing in necessary." Hughes paused, and I could hear a deep breath. "I'm right proud of the way you handled the Irish Mob case. Deputy US Marshal Miller had good words to say about you. It doesn't hurt to be on good terms with the federal government, and you sure enough helped with that. Also, Governor Culberson, bless his heart, is going to be getting some sort of commendation to you. Don't know if anything financial comes with it, but it'll likely fit over your fireplace." Hughes paused again. "Doggone, but I wish I'd been there to see you in action at that backroom ambush. You are of steady character and a first-rate Texas Ranger. You'd do your dad proud."

"Thanks kindly, Captain. I appreciate your offer. You can be sure I'll keep it in mind should the need arise."

As I hung up, Cassie walked in. "Did it go well, Lucas?"

I nodded. "He left the door open anytime I wished to return. I think he knows me better than I know myself."

"Well, he sure doesn't know you like I know you," she cooed, slipping her arms around my shoulders and nearly devouring me with her kiss.

As word spread about my defeating the Irish Mob up in Dallas, I was no longer *persona non gratia*. Folks teased me about how easily I could be taken for an outlaw, since I'd played my part so well. It concerned me how easily folks could be swayed. After a stellar couple of years as a Texas Ranger and fathered by a legendary Texas Ranger, I was shocked at how quickly folks might turn on anyone straying from the straight and narrow life. Many laughed it off; however, I wouldn't soon forget who were quickest to believe the worst of me.

NINETEEN
BANDITS

CAPTAIN HUGHES' concerns about the revolutionists lurking in Mexico caught my attention. We were a mere hundred miles from the border. Any ranch within a four- or five-day ride of the Rio Grande was a possible target for revolutionaries raising money by rustling and selling livestock. I recalled my cousin Red John Dunn sharing the story of the posse he helped pull together back on Good Friday in March of 1875 to fight off Mexican revolutionaries that had invoked Cheno Cortina's name in a series of attacks around Corpus Christi.

Red John's posse freed hostages and chased off the bandits until the posse ran out of ammunition. But the days preceding the Mexican raids were wrought with murder and mayhem, as Texans were robbed and murdered by the revolution-driven bandits. The Good Friday Raid, as they dubbed it, contributed to setting back relations between Whites and Mexicans for many years. That was nearly two dozen years ago. Today, Mexico continues to spawn revolutionaries dissatisfied with their lives enough to violently overthrow their government.

I had read that folks were frustrated with their existence under President Porfirio Diaz. He served term after term, much to the chagrin of those who envisioned succeeding him. Diaz's longtime political adviser Matias Romero had passed away a year ago. Romero had sought to strengthen Mexico's ties with the United States after the Spanish-American War. US foreign policy was shifting toward a stronger version of the Monroe Doctrine. With Romero's death, the Diaz administration's striving for greater US investment in Mexico quickly waned, and rival political factions developed. The trade climate gradually became hostile and contributed to a floundering economy in which Mexican citizens struggled economically. The people became easy prey for revolutionary firebrands. All the factions required funding, and South Texas was seen as a treasure to be plundered.

I had a copy of the Corpus Christi Caller-Times before me as I sipped fresh-brewed coffee and munched on a bear sign.

Cassie sat down opposite me, savoring her own coffee.

Sean and Bode played over near the hearth, and the dogs were outside stirring up varmints to their hearts' content.

"Trouble in Mexico?" she asked.

"Seems like they can't live without some sort of revolution," I lamented. "We'll have to have Pedro and Jimmy stay alert." With tens of thousands of acres to watch over, I reckoned it was high time that we hired a third ranch hand. Even with me back to full-time ranching, keeping the place up was a prodigious task.

"Are we going to…?"

"Hire another hand? Looks as though we must."

"I didn't mean hire another hand, Lucas." She batted her eyes at me.

I stood suddenly and threw the newspaper over her. She leaped from her seat, and I chased her around the kitchen. Cassie laughed and shrieked, much to the delight of Sean and Bode. I caught her, but not too quickly, and swept her into my arms. I kissed her and set her down. "Later, you temptress," I then bellowed with my chest thrust out. The boys were convulsing with laughter at their folks' antics.

"Ha, Lucas Dunn! I happen to have news for you, sir!" she said with hands on her hips and a decidedly enticing look.

"Ha, yourself!" I retorted.

Now, Cassie grew serious.

That stopped me in my tracks. I gave her a quizzical look.

"You're going to be a father again," she finally said and threw herself at me.

I held her off for a moment and gazed into her eyes. "Are you sure?"

"My body plays no tricks on this woman, Mr. Rancher," she replied lovingly.

I reckoned that I must have the same abilities as my dad, who fathered ten children. "This is wonderful, sweetheart." I held her tightly.

By now, the boys realized the chase around the kitchen was ended, so they toddled over to join the hug fest. I looked down at them. "I suppose it's time to add another room to this place," I said.

"What if it's twins?" Cassie chided.

I shook my head. "Then we'd better make the new addition a big one just in case," I responded.

Life at Heaven's Gate Ranch was certainly looking up. My cousin Patrick was raising longhorns out on the northernmost seventy-five miles of Padre Island outside of Corpus Christi. His efforts had opened Corpus to the cattle trade. With Uriah Lott talking of building a rail line he called the St. Louis, Brownsville, and Mexican or SLBM railroad, the market was now tantalizingly close for South Texas ranchers. I wondered whether those revolutionaries stirring things up in Mexico had this figured out.

I recalled my dad dealing with hiders many years back. These were rustlers who stole cattle simply for their hides and left the carcasses behind to rot in the Texas sun. I'd heard that my cousin Patrick still dealt with hiders occasionally. Of course, they regretted challenging the Duke of Padre Island.

Cassie interrupted my mind rambling. "I think the boys need a nap," she said suggestively. I needed no further persuading.

We managed a couple of trips to Corpus Christi for supplies. Such was the nature of ranch life. I wished there was a railroad from our spread to Corpus, but the trip by wagon tended to provide a period of reflection that was actually much needed. One trip to the city was especially memorable. We stopped by the Cacti & Boots haberdashery to make purchases and visit our friends Scarlett and Carson Walker. We walked in, and I couldn't help but notice a new hire.

"Y'all found some new help, Scarlett," I said, sort of tongue in cheek to the proprietor. She had been saved from a life of prostitution by my dad.

At the familiar sound of my voice, the new hire turned to Cassie and me. "Why, Mr. Dunn, how nice of you to stop by," greeted Lilly. "On your recommendation, the Carsons were good enough to hire me. I'm most grateful."

"Thanks, Luke, for sending her our way. Good help is

hard to find. And congratulations on solving that case in Dallas. Sorry we gave you a hard time," apologized Scarlett.

I introduced Lilly to Cassie and explained the circumstances.

We made small talk, bought a couple of items, and went on our way. I pretty much glowed at having the satisfaction of having helped a young woman out of a life that most likely would not have ended well. I suppose it was an upside of what I strove to be as a Texas Ranger. My dad had instilled that sort of character in me.

Sometimes the things we think on and worry about have a tendency to be prophetic. Perhaps, I was overthinking the possible problems with Mexican bandit gangs. Certainly, President Diaz faced serious problems in Mexico, and they tended to foment trouble in the northernmost Mexican states in part due to their long distance from Mexico City. While bandits might roam north of the Rio Grande, it seemed unlikely that they'd find their way nearly a hundred miles north of the border.

So, I sat in my favorite chair on the gallery stretching across the front of our house, taking final sips of coffee before saddling up and surveying our livestock on the south range. I heard a horse and looked up to see Pedro riding my way. Our best ranch hand and experienced *vaquero* had apparently been up mighty early.

"Got a second, Mr. Dunn?" Pedro asked. He always addressed me respectfully and formally.

I put aside my coffee cup and moved to the railing. "Sure, Pedro. What's up?"

"We're missing at least a dozen head on the south range. That's too many to have simply wandered off." I was always impressed that Pedro spoke near-perfect English with hardly a trace of any Mexican accent.

A litany of cuss words came to mind, but I held my tongue. "Thanks, Pedro. I'll saddle up. Round up Jimmy and we'll mosey out that way." I didn't need to mention arming themselves. This might have been 1899, but it was still the rough and tumble frontier of South Texas. I headed inside to let Cassie know what I was up to.

If bandits were encountered, we'd be between the proverbial rock and a hard place. Rustlers caught in the act could be shot. Capturing them was preferable from a humanizing perspective, but if turned in to the law, they'd be sent back to Mexico only to come back and rustle again. Little wonder that considerable animosity was felt by ranchers against Mexicans.

The Texas Ranger in me yearned to follow the law, and so did the rancher in me, but there were limits. A dozen prime beeves represented a lot of money to Heaven's Gate Ranch, and I didn't take kindly to losing a single one of them. We'd soon be rounding up about five hundred head to send to market before winter hit. The fewer fattened beeves we had to feed through the winter, the better. That being said, we didn't cotton to losing cattle without compensation, as in theft.

I saddled up Tornado, gave Cassie and the boys hugs and kisses, petted Brody and Tess, and led Pedro and Jimmy down the lane toward the south range.

Pedro updated us on what evidence he'd found. A fence had been cut, and the tracks of horses and our cattle headed south.

For the first few miles, we rode with our rifles tucked away in saddle scabbards. It was just a couple of years ago that I'd fended off bandits during my hunt for the mystery vigilante, and we wouldn't be too far from where that occurred. I wondered whether one or more rustlers had remembered the area and done some exploring. The three of us talked about life and ranching, as we made our way to the cut fencing. I mentioned the plan to hire another hand, and both hands were enthusiastically on board with that.

The countryside was best described as a vast grassland dotted with meandering arroyos, stands of mesquite and live oak, and the ubiquitous cacti. There were few places for beeves to hide and plenty of grazing, so it was ideal for raising longhorns. We'd acquired a few head of Angus that we were figuring to begin breeding. I also reckoned to open conversation with Robert Kleberg over at the King Ranch toward acquiring some of his Santa Gertrudis breed. It was my hope to diversify our livestock while seeking the optimum combination of stock. I made a note to my brain to go see Kelberg. In fact, I wondered whether he was dealing with any rustling. With a million or so acres to cover, it was a fair bet that the King Ranch faced problems similar to mine. He had far more ranch hands, but also far more land to protect.

It took about two hours to arrive at the cut fencing Pedro had discovered.

"Whew. There's no question that we've been rustled, men," I said, describing the obvious.

"We going to chase them, boss?" asked Jimmy.

"They're long gone, Jimmy. Even with cattle slowing them down and us chasing them miles at full gallop, we'd be unlikely to catch them before they crossed the Rio Grande." I strove to be serious even though close to laughing at the absurdity of his suggestion of giving chase. Still, my lawman instincts wanted to hunt the rustlers down and exact justice.

Pedro came to my rescue. "Let's repair the fence and head home. The rustlers are too far ahead to catch them."

Jimmy caught on. "Yeah. Guess that makes sense." He turned to me. "Maybe, we can pull a posse together, boss," he suggested.

"I appreciate you wanting to hunt these rustlers down, Jimmy. But, once they're in Mexico, we'd have to back off. International incidents are especially frowned upon after the dust-up with Spain."

We went to work repairing the barbed wire and were soon heading home. I sort of wished my old friend Buffalo Watts was still alive, and surely my dad. They'd have solid advice. I had to admit that Jimmy's idea of a posse sounded pretty good. The great challenge, aside from venturing into Mexico, would be where the rustlers went. They'd surely get the cattle sold and then disappear among the people and villages of northern Mexico.

We arrived back at the barn just before sunset. We still had plenty of beeves on our ranges, but the loss of a dozen cut into our profits. While occasional livestock losses from illness, accidents, wolves, or mountain lions were expected, the purposeful theft of cattle was intolerable.

I thought about visiting Sheriff McTiernan, but figured it was fruitless, as I'd likely receive no help. Even the political influences of Archer Parr and Stephen Powers weren't up to dealing with incursions by Mexican bandits. Heaven forbid that they should risk their political ambitions over a few stolen head of cattle.

Cassie and the boys were waiting on the gallery for us.

"We've been rustled," I confirmed.

"And?" she queried.

I shrugged. "There's a lot of range to cover. We could send an army down there, and they still might steal our beeves." The frustration I felt colored Cassie's expression. "We'll ride down that way a bit more often, but there's not much more we can do. I'll go talk with Kleberg and see how he's handling it." I already knew how my cousin Patrick dealt with rustlers, and it wasn't pretty. They never saw Mexico again, though he'd never admit—nor would anyone else—to having done anything to them.

Next morning, I was sitting enjoying my usual coffee before heading out to inspect our ranges, when I caught the sound of a horse galloping up the lane toward our house. Before the rider even came into view, I'd grabbed the Winchester that always stood just inside our front door. I wasn't featuring surprises these days with rustlers running around.

"Mr. Dunn! Mr. Dunn!" called out the rider, as he approached. He pulled up his well-lathered mount in front of me in a great cloud of dust. "Greasers done captured the Brody family. Holding them for ransom!" he yelled.

I recognized the young man as Petey Gulbreath who managed the livery stable in Nuecestown. "Ease up, Petey. Get down and explain slowly."

Cassie heard the commotion and emerged to stand beside me.

Petey dismounted and took a deep breath. "About a dozen of them damned greasers have taken the Brody family. Rode up in broad daylight, threatened them with guns, and want money for their safe return."

"How long ago?" I asked.

"Maybe four or five hours, Mr. Dunn," responded the near-breathless teen.

"Where they holding them?"

"The old Richardson barn near Nuecestown," he replied.

"You say a dozen. No more? No less?"

"Twelve exactly, Mr. Dunn. And lots of guns. Wearin' them bandolier things. They keep hootin' and hollerin' about some fella named Reyes who's against the head honcho in Mexico."

Cassie gave me a questioning look, as she wondered whether I was going to risk life and limb pursuing a bandit gang.

I smiled and turned to Cassie. "Fear not, sweetheart. I'm not going to play hero." I'd read about Bernardo Reyes opposing Diaz, but not to the extent of fomenting revolution. These kidnappers had to have gone rogue. "Petey, you go tell my cousins Red John, Nick, and his son John, and my cousin Matt to gather at the entrance arch to Heaven's Gate at Noon today and come well-armed. Then tell Sheriff McTiernan what's happening." Red John and Matt had been Texas Rangers, so they would be experienced at dealing with these sorts of scenarios. The Good Friday Raid back in 1875 that Red John was involved with was bigger than this, so he'd be a huge help. I sent Petey on his way.

By this time, Pedro and Jimmy had arrived on the scene. "You need us, Mr. Dunn?" asked Pedro.

"You're under no obligation," I replied.

"You can count on us, boss," contributed Jimmy.

"Pack plenty of ammunition," I advised and pulled Cassie back inside our house.

"Lucas, I thought you were done with this," she reminded me.

"You and the boys could be the next victims, Cassie. We've got to deal with this."

She sighed. "You going to arrest them?"

"Doesn't matter. They're trespassers, not American citizens."

"Really?" she challenged.

"I'll try to free the Brodys peacefully. Maybe we can just

run the bandits off." I tried to be reassuring, though wasn't so sure we could avoid bloodshed. I figured it'd be worth a try if it saved folks from being hurt or killed.

Cassie sighed and hugged me. "Just get yourself back here safely, Lucas."

It was getting nigh to Noon when Pedro, Jimmy, and I headed for the archway to Heaven's Gate Ranch. We said nary a word, as each of us was absorbed in personal thoughts of the possible dangers lying ahead. We were first to arrive at the gateway.

"May as well rest our hosses, men," I suggested.

We dismounted and stood around at loose ends. What if my cousins didn't show up?

Horses soon appeared on the road from Corpus. It looked to be a couple of my cousins. I recalled that Nick was well into his sixties, so I wasn't surprised that he was absent. Red John was no spring chicken, but he and his handlebar mustache were joining us. Nick's son John Dunn rode along, as well as another Texas Ranger alumnus cousin Rut Evans, and my cousin Matt Dunn. It was looking to be seven against twelve. With four of us former Texas Rangers, the odds were better than ever for us.

"Y'all heard what's happened?" I said by way of opening a conversation.

"Back in '75, the Mexicans had the good sense to release most of their hostages before we took it to them. Only that overanxious George Swank took a bullet. Lots of lead buzzed around, but no others killed on either side. We just about ran out of ammo. My experience is that when the bullets fly, the Mexicans will run like scared rabbits."

"You want to lead this, Red John?" I was willing to defer to his experience.

Red John guffawed. "You kidding me? You been grabbing the headlines lately, solving this and that case. This is your baby, Junior."

I hadn't been called Junior in a while. It was sort of a deference to my dad. I did feel his presence among us.

"I agree," contributed Rut.

There was a round of yeas. I was the leader of the posse. "Petey said that they're holed up in the old abandoned barn on the Richardson homestead. Not sure how long they'll stay there. I understand they're looking for money." At that, I wondered what American was figuring to negotiate with the bandits. "Guess we might be trading lead instead of dollars."

"What do you have in mind, boss?" asked Jimmy.

"Guess we'll try the white flag first," I temporized.

"That didn't help your cousin Lawrence back in the War of Northern Aggression," noted Red John. "Poor SOB went in under a white flag to dicker with Mexican rustlers on behalf of the Rebs, and the cowards shot him in the back."

"You propose something else?" I challenged.

"Just sayin'," he replied. "White flag is likely the best way to start. Whoever carries the flag gets to see their defenses."

I looked from man to man. "I know a little Mex. I'll talk to them." Cassie wouldn't be very happy with me. I kept in mind that a family was being held hostage, and their lives depended on us. "I recall that there's a knoll a few yards out and above the barn. I expect it would be the best vantage point to get things started. If we're attacked, we'd be defending the higher ground."

We headed for Nuecestown. We were surely a ragtag-looking bunch, if ever there was one. I was far and away the biggest and youngest, cutting a fine figure on my Appaloosa stallion. It was a tad chilly, so I wore a buckskin jacket. Of course, I carried my Smith & Wesson revolver and my Winchester carbine with plenty of ammunition. Pedro wore this big sombrero that he cottoned to and had a serape slung over his shoulders and hiding an old Colt Peacemaker. He did carry one of the new Winchesters that I'd purchased for each of the ranch hands.

My cousin Red John was slender as a rail, but anyone could see that he was tough as nails. Under a broad-brimmed felt hat and behind a red handlebar mustache, he looked every bit the part of a throwback Texas Ranger. He wore a wool vest, a Colt revolver stick in a holster at his side, and a Henry repeating rifle. Jimmy? Well, he looked like most any ranch hand, though he had a bandolier across his chest. I reckoned he'd never run out of bullets to feed his Winchester.

My cousin Rut was dressed in a navy-colored wool jacket that hid a wallop-packing Colt New Service .45 caliber revolver with a six-inch barrel. Cousin John Dunn looked more like a banker than a rancher, much less a posse member. He had a reputation of being as tough a man as ever walked the earth. John wore a three-piece dark gray wool suit. He'd just joined the board of the Alice National Bank, so he had added banking duties to running a ranch. Ragtag just about summed us up. It felt as though there was enough firepower among us to take on an army. Those Mexican bandits had no idea what they were up against.

TWENTY
WHITE FLAG

IT WAS about a ten-mile ride to the old Richardson barn west of Nuecestown. We'd been blessed with a clear, crisp autumn day. By our reckoning, the weather wouldn't matter to the bandits. We soon arrived at the knoll above the barn, as I'd suggested, and made enough noise for the bandits to realize they had company.

"Hola, amigos!" I shouted.

"Aye, gringos!" came a response from the shadows within the barn.

I heard a meek female cry for help, followed by a slap and thud. It sounded as though one of the bandits had struck Mrs. Brody.

"Queremos parlamentar!" I called down at them that we wanted to parley.

A couple of the bandits paraded the hostages out for us to see. The Mexicans stayed hidden behind the Brody family as though they were shields. *"Tienes dinero?"* hollered the apparent bandit leader. I couldn't help but notice a few rifles bristling from the barn. Petey had been right in estimating a dozen bandits.

"Hablemos," I responded, saying we wanted to talk. "*Quién es tu líder*?" I wanted the name of whom I was going to parley with. I tied a large piece of white cloth to the muzzle of my Winchester. It occurred to me that I'd better hope the bandits knew what the white flag meant. It sure enough didn't matter now, as I urged Tornado a few steps toward the barn. I was now a target. In the back of my mind lingered Red John's story of my cousin Lawrence being murdered by Mexican bandits despite carrying a white flag.

A Mexican in a black suit embroidered with red and gold sequined shapes and wearing a wide sombrero emerged from the barn on a black horse. Bandoliers filled with bullets crossed his chest. His spurs featured especially large rowels. The man surely was a fancified example for wardrobes of revolutionary leaders. He rode forward under a white flag.

We met about twenty feet apart. "*Habla inglés*?" I asked. While I understood the Mexican language fairly well, I much preferred English.

A devilish, tooth-filled smile emerged from between the man's mustache and beard. "Yes, *gringo. Muy bien. Prefiero el español, pero hablamos en inglés.* I am Carlos Arturo Mayor, leader of the Revolution. Viva Mexico!" He paused. "Who are you?"

"Well, *buenas dias, Señor* Mayor. My name is Luke Dunn. Me and most of my friends back yonder are former Texas Rangers come to relieve you of those fine innocent folks you're parading. *Comprendo*?"

"It cost you *mucho dinero, Señor* Dunn," replied Mayor, brimming with confidence. Were he walking about, he'd likely be strutting. His black gelding pranced a little as though showing off for the men in the barn. His black saddle decorated with silver conchos added a touch of glitter.

"*Cuánto*?" I asked.

"Five thousand United States dollars for the Revolution!" responded the bandit leader.

"What happens, if we don't pay?" I ventured, though I figured that I knew the answer.

"Nice family die, *muy muerto*"

It was my turn to smile, and it wasn't a kind one. "Well, we don't reckon to pay you any money. In fact, you can send the Brody family out to us right now, and we will permit you to return to Mexico unharmed." I nodded toward the hostages. "Oh, and if any of the Brody family die, you will all die. Are you ready to die, *Señor* Mayor? The coyotes and buzzards await your answer."

The bandit leader gazed deeply into my eyes. If he expected me to cough up money, he'd been taken quite off guard. What he caught instead was the cold steeled visage of a lawman who'd been down this sort of road before. He glanced nervously over his shoulder at his comrades, then up at the firepower aimed at him from atop the knoll. He was in a deep quandary. He hadn't expected having to deal with a strong gringo, and he'd pumped his bandit gang up with visions of easy money. He surely didn't want to back down, yet to yield to my demand might cause his men to mutiny. Harming the hostages meant death to him and his bandits. "I talk with my *amigos*," said Mayor.

I backed Tornado up the hill with the muzzle of my *flagpole* aimed toward the barn. There'd be no back shooting.

"What'd he say?" asked Red John.

"He is Carlos Mayor, and he's not excited about the prospect of dying if harm comes to the Brody family. He expected easy money. Now, he's talking it over with his men."

"What do you think, Mr. Dunn?" asked Pedro.

"I don't think he wants to die. That is what I think," I replied with a self-assured grin.

We all turned our attention to the loud squabbling going on inside the barn. It continued for several minutes, then all grew quiet.

"Some argue to fight," warned Pedro.

We heard horses galloping out from the far side of the old barn. It was three of the bandits, including Mayor. The Brody family appeared in the barn doorway. The bandits prodded them with their rifles and forced them to begin to slowly walk up the hill toward us.

They'd walked barely twenty feet when I spotted rifle muzzles reemerge from the barn.

"Get Down!" I hollered to Brody. "Get down!"

A volley of rifle fire from the barn shattered the air.

The Brody family dove into the dirt. I heard a scream. At least one Brody had been hit. A hail of bullets buzzed over their heads.

"Lay it into the damned fools!" I ordered.

We delivered a withering fire into the barn. While we lay protected by the sandy loam soil of our knoll, the rotted and worn wood siding of the barn offered little cover for the bandits. Moans and screams were soon emanating from within the shaky old structure. Thankfully, the Brody family stayed glued to the earth while lead flew over their heads.

Shooting from the barn ceased. A deadly silence prevailed.

"Hold fire!" I called out.

A couple of whimpers and moans could be heard from inside the barn. Two bandits, one obviously wounded, galloped away from the far side of the barn.

"*Alguien vivo allí*?" I hollered as to whether anyone in the barn was alive.

"*Ayuda*," came a weak reply.

It was a call for help. Was it trickery?

"Rut, you and I will circle around to approach the barn from the other side." We took off at a run. Thanks to the knoll, we were out of the line of sight of anyone inside.

Rut and I entered cautiously from the far side and were shocked at the scene before us. Light streamed in from bullet holes in the barn walls, casting a macabre pall of shadows on the dead and dying.

Five bandits lay dead, and two were seriously wounded and crying their hearts out for help.

With Rut watching my back, I strode over to the first wounded bandit. He'd been shot twice in the belly. His guts were exposed and he was dying. "*Que lástima,*" I said. "*Vaya con Dios, hombre.*" He looked back at me with pleading eyes and breathed his last.

I turned to the last remaining bandit. He too had been shot multiple times and was at death's door. There was nothing we could do. Rut and I watched him pass away before our eyes.

I looked around the barn. It reeked of gun smoke, sweat, and human waste. Two horses lay dead, and I put a wounded one out of its misery. With the barn secure, we quickly ran to the Brody family, still clinging to Texas soil. "It's okay, folks. Y'all are safe," I called out.

Mr. Brody and the two children stood, but the mother lay in the grass bleeding from a bullet wound.

Don Brody kneeled beside his wife. He looked up at me helplessly.

I looked over his shoulder. I saw a deep flesh wound across her shoulder. It didn't appear to be life-threatening. "She's going to live, Mr. Brody. Let's get her to the doc."

The rest of my posse led their horses and Tornado down the hill toward us.

"They all done in?" asked Red John.

I nodded sort of ruefully then got a hold of myself. "Everybody reload." My Texas Ranger cousins had done this automatically, but Pedro and Jimmy needed reminding. If Mayor found his machismo, he might return and make trouble.

Mr. Brody looked up at me through tear-filled eyes. "Bless you all. They were talking about killing us."

"Pedro, Jimmy, let's get Mrs. Brody to the doc."

"There's no doc in Nuecestown anymore, boss," said Jimmy.

"Damn. Well, go find a wagon and get her to Corpus. Mr. Brody, keep your bandana pressed against her wound to stop the bleeding."

My orders had the effect of moving Don Brody to action. It was important that he get past the shock of all that had happened. So, I put him to work stopping the bleeding of his wife's wound while his young sons ran off with Jimmy to help fetch a wagon.

We were now standing around congratulating ourselves. We hadn't even thought of the mess in the barn that would need cleaning up. I was about to thank everyone and send them home, when we heard galloping horses headed our way.

Mexican revolutionary Carlos Arturo Mayor hadn't quit after all. "Aiyee!" came the cries of he and five companions. Apparently, a couple of local disgruntled Mexicans had joined him to swell his revolutionary force. They were charging toward us full tilt with rifles blazing.

We all hit the dirt and began returning fire.

We were quickly surrounded by dust, horses, and gunfire. Praise God that rifles are next to worthless in a battle at close range. They become little more than clubs. Mayor and his bandits were pressed to get beads on targets. Our revolvers went into action. Within seconds, six saddles were emptied. Three horses suffered mortal wounds, Mayor and three attackers lay dead, and two wounded bandits stood on wobbly legs with hands raised high.

One of the bandits dropped to his knees and aimed his rifle at me. It clicked on an empty chamber. A bullet from Red John felled him like a sack of potatoes. The last bandit pleaded desperately for his life. He was bleeding profusely from wounds to his head and chest. The poor soul cried for his mother and his God. Mortally wounded, he keeled over and met his Maker.

We took stock of our situation. My cousins Matt and John had suffered superficial bullet wounds. They'd join Mrs. Brody for the ride to Corpus Christi.

"Thanks. Thanks so very much." Don Brody fairly gushed with heartfelt gratitude.

"Just being neighborly," I understated with a friendly smile and tip of my hat.

Red John gave me an appraising look. "Damned if you're not every bit your dad and more, Lucas Dunn. I'd be proud to serve in any Ranger company you led."

Those were huge words of compliment, and I could feel myself blush.

"You know what they say," he offered.

"You mean once a Ranger, always a Ranger?" I said good-naturedly. "We'll see, Red John Dunn. We'll see."

"I guess anyone not going to Corpus can go home. Thanks for your help. I suppose it'll be up to the fine folks of Nuecestown to clean this all up before the coyotes and buzzards arrive." I sure wasn't fancying the idea of pulling smelly, dead bodies from the now bullet-riddled barn. As if to punctuate my sentiments, one wall of the barn and part of the roof seized the moment to collapse. It was a fitting ending to the day's adventure.

I reloaded my Winchester just to feel secure and because

it was what I was taught to do. Thinking back, it had been good advice to have everybody reload their weapons after the initial battle.

As we loaded the wagon and were fixing to leave, along rode none other than Sheriff McTiernan. He rode straight to me, surveying the scene as he approached.

"John," I said. "How good of you to stop by." I could have been tougher on him, but he had helped me with past Texas Ranger cases, especially the murders on the Guadalupe River.

"Whew! What went down, Luke?" he asked.

"Red John here would tell you it was a curtain call for the Good Friday Raid back in '75. Bunch of wannabe Mexican revolutionaries took the Brody family here hostage and wanted money for their release. We pulled a posse together and rescued them."

"Sorry that I couldn't have been here sooner," lamented McTiernan with genuine concern.

"Well, John, if you don't mind. We've done the heavy lifting. It'd be a big help, if you could find some folks to clean this all up. Shame we can't cart all these dead Mexicans back to Chihuahua."

McTiernan recognized that he was getting his just desserts for being a late arrival. "You go home, Luke. I'll take care of cleaning things up." He turned to Don Brody. "I hope your wife recovers fully, Mr. Brody. Glad y'all are safe." McTiernan wanted another term as sheriff.

I took a final look around, mounted Tornado, and headed home with Pedro. Jimmy would drive the wagon to Corpus Christi and be home the next morning. As we headed up the road toward Heaven's Gate Ranch, I turned to Pedro. "Never ceases to amaze me how hopelessness makes men so susceptible to impassioned causes. No matter that death may await; that families are split asunder.

Every one of those supposed revolutionaries back there had mothers and fathers. Might have had wives and children. Now, there are widows and orphans. Was some hopeless cause worth dying for?"

Pedro nodded his acknowledgment of what was most likely a deep truth.

"That Kyle McClintock had the evil fire of envy in his belly. It wed him to evil deeds. I knew his ma and pa. They were good folks, but their seed was nourished by self-imposed misery, pain, and suffering. Garth Jones was dedicated to killing me. He too was captive to motivations inspired by evil. The Grim Reaper obliged them with death's justice."

"*Señor* Dunn, you're talking heavy today," observed Jimmy.

I smiled grimly. "As a lawman, I dealt with the heavy side of life, Jimmy. I suppose that as a rancher, I still do."

"Those men were *muy loco,*" contributed Pedro. "My people are Mexican Tejanos. We're very happy here in America. *No entiendo a los revolucionarios. Esta muy loco.*"

"I don't understand them either, Pedro. There must be peaceful ways to get governments to change." I gave Tornado an extra nudge. "Hey, maybe we'll be home in time for dinner. You come join Cassie and me." I didn't invite the hands to dine with us very often. There was an unwritten code that hands didn't mix socially with ranch owners. We didn't totally ascribe to that. We were a family with a modest-sized ranch that was generally profitable. To that end, we appreciated the hard work and loyalty of the men who worked for us.

I wondered whether my life would ever reach a time of what some folks might call normalcy. Right this minute, I just wanted a good meal and to love my wife and children.

TWENTY-ONE
GROWING THE RANCH

"ARE you going after Mexican revolutionaries or longhorns today?" joked Cassie, as she placed a plate piled high with eggs, sausage, and biscuits before me.

What could I do but laugh? "I think I'll stick with beeves. I may visit Robert Kleberg in the next day or so and see whether he'll part with some of his Santa Gertrudis breed. They're tough like longhorns but a lot meatier."

"Sounds like a good idea. I understand that they're raising some fine Quarter Horses at the King Ranch," offered Cassie.

"You're right about that, sweetheart. I'm not so sure we can compete with them, but it might be fun to try. Cowboys are looking for stamina, speed, and agility. If we bought a couple of breeders, we could mate them with mustangs. I understand the hybrid produces a tougher Quarter Horse while maintaining the speed and agility. They're ideal for working cattle."

"Would you like more coffee?" she asked.

"You might brew a bit more. I'm going to chat with a cowpoke Jimmy met in Corpus while helping the Brody family. He worked as a wrangler for the King Ranch. We'll see whether he fits our needs."

"What's his name?" Cassie asked.

"Carswell. His name is Jake Carswell."

Cassie rubbed her chin thoughtfully, then folded her arms. "I've heard some of the women I chat with talking about a man of that name. They say that he enjoys the ladies and fine whisky."

"Many men do," I responded.

"I mean…" She blushed.

"Soiled doves," I said, finishing her sentence.

Cassie nodded. "I hear tell that he's handsome, too."

"Can't be holding that against him, though his personal habits may be a concern." I finished up the last bites of my breakfast. "I'm going to head to the barn and see to Tornado while I wait for Carswell."

Cassie nodded. "If he knocks at our door, I'll send him along."

We kissed. I took a final swallow of coffee and headed to the barn.

I'd just finished currying Tornado, when Jake Carswell strode into the barn. He was of short stature, compact and muscular, and, as the women opined, a handsomeness about him. I towered over him.

"Mr. Dunn?" he inquired.

"Howdy. You must be Jake Carswell. Jimmy Donovan told me a bit about you," I said, slipping a glove from my hand and extending it to Carswell. He had a firm grip. My dad had taught me that a man's handshake grip was a window to his character.

"Jimmy said you were looking for a new hand," said Carswell.

"That's true. Let's mosey over to the corral out there and chat a bit."

Carswell followed me to the corral beside the barn. I put a boot on the lower rail and gazed at a bay stallion prancing around.

"Good looking," observed Carswell, running his eyes over the bay.

"I hear that you worked for Bob Kleberg?" I queried.

"You heard correctly, Mr. Dunn," he replied.

"You leave of your own accord?" I pressed.

"It's a big spread. Mr. Kleberg employs lots of *vaqueros*. Many are great at what they do. It was too crowded for me."

I reckoned this was an honest answer. "You get along with folks?"

Carswell looked from the bay to me. "Mostly. To be honest, I had a couple of spats with some *vaqueros*. They were a club of sorts, and I was too *gringo* for them." He turned back to the bay. "He saddle broke?"

I nodded. "Bought him from a cousin. He's pure mustang. Reckon to breed him with Quarter Horses."

"There's a few Quarter Horses at the King Ranch. They do a good job breeding them," noted Carswell.

The bay walked over to me and let me stroke his nose. To be honest, he was just recently saddle broke. He tended to be a tad frisky.

I walked to the corral gate and opened it. "Come on in, Mr. Carswell," I invited.

"You can call me Jake, Mr. Dunn," he said and followed me into the corral.

The bay stallion looked askance at Carswell. In addition to handshakes, I tended to judge my hired hands by how they related to livestock. I waited to see how Carswell interacted with the bay.

"Hey," he said gently and extended his hand.

The bay snorted and tossed his head. He looked at me, then at Carswell. Another snort, and he placed his snout in Carswell's hand. The prospective hire patted the bay's neck and was soon hugging him. I liked what I was seeing.

"I pay thirty-five a month plus space in the bunkhouse and three squares a day. Is yonder cayuse yours?"

Carswell nodded. "I made forty at King Ranch."

"We're a considerably smaller operation. If you prove out, we can make adjustments."

Carswell gave my offer some thought. "Any time off?"

I laughed. "We schedule that. Nuecestown is close but dying, but Corpus and Alice offer plenty of entertainment."

"I got used to Kingsville and Falfurrias. I reckon Corpus offers a bit more," Carswell said with a laugh.

"They even have running water in Corpus Christi," I chided.

"I understand you were a Texas Ranger, Mr. Dunn," Carswell inquired. "I hear tell that you solved some tough cases.

"You heard right, Jake," I confirmed. "It's still the wild west out there on occasion. We had to raise a posse just the other day. You have any experience with law or military?"

"No. If you're asking whether I can defend myself, rest assured that I can."

"Well, you met Jimmy. Let's introduce you to my other cowboy, Pedro."

"Pedro Martinez?" asked Carswell.

"The very same," I responded.

"I know him well. I got a little tipsy a couple of years back in Falfurrias, and Pedro put a much-deserved licking on me. I like the man."

"Well, if he likes you, you're hired, Jake," I said.

By chance, Pedro strolled into view.

"Pedro!" I called out.

He eased over to Carswell and me. "You going to hire this bum, *Señor* Dunn?" he said with a laugh. "He's okay. I keep him straight."

"Welcome aboard, Jake." We shook hands.

I wasn't able to strike a deal with Kleberg for his Santa Gertrudis beeves, but I managed to get better educated about Quarter Horses. The King Ranch was having quite a bit of success raising the breed, and I confirmed that there was plenty of opportunity in raising and selling them. It was important to keep track of the lineage of the horses that were bred, as breeding consistency significantly enhanced value.

Pedro, Jimmy, and Jake worked well together, so I felt optimistic about raising Quarter Horses in addition to beeves. I set my cousin Larry Dunn to work finding me a good deal on a couple of Quarter Horse stallions and a mare. I wanted to mate a Quarter Horse mare with the bay stallion I'd recently had saddle broke, and I had a few mustang mares to breed with the stallions.

Thanksgiving was drawing near, and I figured to make it special for family, friends, and hands. I ordered up four turkeys from an outfit in Corpus Christi. These weren't wild turkeys as could be found out on our range, but domestically raised birds fattened up for Thanksgiving feasting. With all the fixings and so much to be grateful for, Thanksgiving would be especially celebratory this year. I sent Jimmy to fetch the birds.

As anyone might imagine, plucking and prepping, and

cooking four big turkeys was a prodigious task. I had the good sense to take on the preparation with the help of Pedro, Jimmy, and Jake. I even built a smoker oven behind the house, as there was no way the oven in our kitchen could handle it along with all the other Thanksgiving dishes.

Jimmy took a serious whack with a ladle from Cassie, when he tried to steal an apple pie sitting on the kitchen windowsill to cool. I could hardly blame him as the sweet, fruity aroma wafted its way to the bunkhouse.

Thanksgiving finally came around. We hosted a crowd at our table. Aside from Cassie and the boys, there were Cassie's mom and dad, my mom, and our three ranch hands. No one was going hungry.

I'm not a church-going fellow, but I worship God and Jesus. So it was that I got to kick off the feast with a blessing. Then, it was time to dig in. The table was piled high. Turkey, potatoes, green beans, corn, baked rolls, and cranberries were topped off with scrumptious desserts featuring the aforementioned apple pie, along with two blueberry pies. The Pilgrims and Wampanoag Indians would have loved our feast. We drank the obligatory coffee, but apple cider and beer served to enhance the consumption. When it was all over, we sat over at the hearth and sang and told tall tales. Sean and Bode were yet too young to appreciate the stories, but I was sure some of the impromptu acting made an unforgettable impression.

When all was over and bellies were so full folks could no longer move, I said a few words about what we had planned for the coming year. "We'll mostly hunker down for the winter and take care of making and repairing things that can be worked on indoors. No telling what sort of weather we'll have." I looked around at the faces surrounding me. Sean and Bode were asleep and Cassie was getting drowsy. The hands and our parents tried to be attentive, while the pups chowed down on what scraps they could find.

"The addition of a bedroom to this place is underway, and I'm fixing to build a second barn strictly for our Quarter Horse breeding. We did right well at market with the beeves we sold a couple of weeks back, so I hope to grow the herd substantially next year. We'll look into Herefords." Now, the ranch hands and our parents were struggling to stay awake. I shrugged. This was a losing battle. "Oh, and a third Dunn child will join us in the spring." Eyes popped open. We hadn't shared the news before this. Everyone was wide awake and congratulations filled the air.

Well, everyone recovered from the Thanksgiving feast. Winter followed right quickly on the heels of a mild autumn. If we expected winter to follow suit, we were sadly mistaken. A blizzard swept across South Texas just a couple of days before Christmas. I expect it was a harbinger of what was to come. The good news was that our ranch spread on mostly flat prairies, so snowdrifts were no serious problem. But strong winds howled across Heaven's Gate Ranch for days, blowing ice and snow at you instead of on you.

We were fortunate to not be out in the storm, but worried about livestock. The move to send several hundred head to market back in September turned out to have been a fortuitous one, given that it reduced our potential losses. We'd laid out plenty of hay before the blizzard, so I was confident that our beeves would be well fed. Temperatures had plummeted, so we did our best to keep ice from forming in water holes around the ranch.

Once the storms abated, Pedro, Jimmy, Jake, and I began venturing out to see how our beeves had fared. We did lose a few older, weaker cattle. The longhorns were amazingly tough.

We endured the harsh winter that ushered in the turn of the century and hopes for the coming year. The snow melts meant that lush grasses would feed our beeves and horses, and we'd begin breeding Quarter Horses. Somehow, we managed to complete the bedroom addition to our house and even began work on a new barn strictly for breeding horses. We'd be welcoming another Dunn to the household any day.

TWENTY-TWO
ROGUE APACHE

I WAS RIDING fence one early March morning, when Jake came riding in looking ready to bust with some sort of story.

"Mr. Dunn, I heard something terrible yesterday in Corpus," he began.

The newspaper hadn't reached the ranch just yet, so I was curious as to what fresh news he was bringing. "What's it about, Jake?"

"A couple of cowpokes from Falfurrias were talking about King Ranch cattle being rustled by Apache. The Indians are led by a fellow named Chato."

"Damn, Jake. Here it is 1900, and we're worrying about Indian attacks?" I asked incredulously. I recalled my dad dealing with Comanche, but I figured those days were long gone. "Did they say how big this Chato fellow's band is?"

"They claimed that horse tracks indicated a dozen warriors. They were pretty snockered, so might have exaggerated."

"You thinking the Apache might get to us?" I asked.

"If they can get away with stealing from the King Ranch, we'd be easy prey," he replied.

"Let's all gather up around dinner this evening and discuss it, Jake. Thanks for the heads up." I urged him to ride off and returned to fence riding. It had been a good day so far as our fences, as there was no cut barbed wire.

As I rode on, I cogitated on what I knew of the Apache in Texas. It had been twenty years, since Victorio and Nana had been vanquished. No one especially worried about Indians anymore. Nearly all were ensconced on reservations. The Redman had ultimately succumbed to a combination of reduced food supply, disease, a strong US military, and sheer numbers of White settlers. Reservation conditions were inadequate at best, and Indians were slow to adapt. It should have been no surprise that there would be those who rebelled at the travesties wrought against the proud Indian.

Nana, a Chiricahua Apache, turned out to be the toughest of the tribe. He'd married Geronimo's sister and fought with Cuchillo Negro and Mangas Coloradas. He joined Victorio in battle until that chief was killed by the Mexican Army at the Battle of Tres Castillos in 1880. Despite fighting on, Nana was ultimately captured and spent his final years in prison or under military custody.

While all the Apache chiefs put up good fights, they all ultimately succumbed. That did not prevent them from becoming revered, even seen as martyrs, by young Apache men who felt disenfranchised. Chato, translated as the Cat, was one of them. His name was quite apropos, as he seemed to be able to sneak catlike in and out of Texas at will.

★★

Cassie joined us in the bunkhouse as we gathered to discuss Chato.

"I thought the Apache were finished, Lucas," pondered Cassie aloud.

"I thought so, too, until Jake brought me the news this morning that the King Ranch had been rustled by Apache under some rogue named Chato."

"Pardon, Mrs. Dunn, ma'am," interjected Jimmy. He turned to me. "You figuring we'll be rustled, too?"

"Shucks, if bandits can find their way this far to wreak their brand of trouble, why not Apache?" waxed Pedro thoughtfully. "My cousins near the border say Apache unhappy."

"There's only a handful of us. If this Chato has a dozen warriors, we're seriously outnumbered. "There's not much we can do but stay alert. From here on, we ride the range in pairs. If you hear anything new from neighbors or folks in Corpus or Alice, let us know as soon as possible. It goes without saying to be sure your guns are loaded and in good working order."

Everybody nodded.

Cassie and I headed back to the house. We were about halfway between the bunkhouse and our house, when she stopped. "Lucas! It's time, Lucas!" Child number three was on its way.

We shuffled off to the house, and I managed to help her to our bedroom. Sean and Bode were silently observing their parents' strange behavior.

"Sean, you and Bode feed Brody and Tess," I urged. Bode couldn't say a word yet, but Sean had begun to talk enough to know what I was saying. He dutifully went about the task, while I scooped up an armful of towels and began warming water on the stove. Amazingly, I was quite calm.

"Lucas!" came the call from the bedroom.

I was going to help deliver a baby boy or girl into the world. Cassie would be doing the hard part.

Blessedly, Sean and Bode stayed with the dogs.

Coincidentally, my mom showed up. It was confusing for a moment as Sean answered the door.

"Where's your daddy?" asked Mom.

Sean pointed upstairs, and Mom saw the water warming on our stove and quickly put the pieces together. "Baby?" she asked Sean.

He nodded.

I was helping Cassie through her labor pushes as Mom knocked and walked into the room. "May I help?" she asked. This was from a woman who'd brought me and nine others into the world.

"Please," said Cassie and I in unison.

It seemed like another hour had passed, and a baby girl was clinging to Cassie's chest. Mom and I hugged, and she went off to prepare some soup for Cassie. I was hungry, but that hardly mattered.

Cassie was exhausted, but looked up at me from the bed through eyes fighting off sleep. "What shall we name her?" she half whispered.

It was my turn, but I felt she should name our first girl. "You name her, sweetheart."

She looked at me through dreamy eyes. "I like Carolyn. Carolyn Alma Dunn." Her eyelids closed, and she fell asleep.

I lifted Carolyn Alma Dunn from Cassie's chest and loved her with my eyes. Picture a six-foot-three-inch rancher making sure his baby girl's blanket was snug and laying her in a crib. I turned and found my mom watching me.

"Congratulations, son," she said with a sweet motherly smile. "Little Carolyn is a blessing to our family."

What could I do but hug her?

"Good to have another woman around here, too," she added with a laugh.

Another little one in the house sure enough changed the dynamic. With the myriad chores inherent in ranch life, a three-year-old, a two-year-old, and a newborn were a lot for Cassie to handle. It sure was wonderful that our mothers lived close enough to us that they could come help now and then.

So it was, that I was out riding fence one day in early April. Cassie's mother had come by to spend the day helping out. Of course, the real reason was that she loved grand-mothering the children. We were still worried about Apache, so we rode in pairs. Jake was with me this day.

"Maybe, we'll see some Apache today," joked Jake. We'd begun a conversation earlier, when we were saddling up in the barn. We hadn't heard of any recent Apache incursions, and Chato's name hadn't popped up.

"You think they still take scalps?" I chided with an eye to Jake's long, dark hair.

"Pshaw! I reckon to keep my hair," he laughed.

We were still laughing, when I reined in. "Listen," I said. Jake pulled up beside me.

The faint sound of voices was carried to our ears. We were downwind of whoever was talking.

"Sounds like Indian talk," I conjectured.

"Oh hell," replied Jake.

We checked our revolver loads and slipped our Winchesters from their saddle scabbards.

"Might have trouble down where the fence crosses the creek," I opined. "We're downwind. Let's see if we can get close enough to get a count."

We rode forward cautiously, scanning the area for possible lookouts as we drew closer. We halted behind a motte of live oak about a hundred yards from what turned out to be Apache. There were eight of them in view. They were busy cutting the section of fence crossing a creek, exactly where I'd suspected. We scanned the area to be sure there were no sentries.

While we remained downwind, we were too close to even whisper comfortably. We withdrew a hundred yards or so.

"What do you think, Mr. Dunn?" asked Jake.

I was rubbing my chin thoughtfully. Far as I could figure, the Apache had their sights set on four beeves a little way up the creek from where the fence crossed. I thought on my wife and three little ones at home. "Trying to decide whether it's worth the risk, Jake," I responded.

"They're carrying antiques," observed Jake.

I had to agree that we had them significantly outgunned. A looming question was how they'd react, if we attacked? We did have the element of surprise, and they'd soon be burdened with having to drive a handful of longhorns. The Texas Ranger in me was up to taking them on. The lawman and rancher won over the common sense of a man with growing family responsibilities. "Okay, Jake. Let's take it to them. Picket our horses here. We'll go back to that live oak motte and have us some target shooting." This was shades of a couple of years back, when I was hunting the vigilante and fought off a passel of Mexicans.

Jake offered up a broad smile. "I'm with you, Mr. Dunn."

We hitched our cayuses and stealthily walked down to the trees with Winchesters fully loaded.

The Apache were focused on trying to coax the longhorns through the break they'd cut in the fence. The beasts were thirsty and causing the Indians no end of trouble.

"You take the two on the left, Jake." With that, I levered a round, aimed, and squeezed off the first shot. An Apache went rigid, then fell from his pony.

Jake opened fire.

Between us, three Apache took bullets before the rest of the band could react. Cattle-be-damned, the remaining hostiles took off at a full gallop. I nailed one more, as they sped off.

"Whew! Nice shooting," observed Jake.

"I don't think we'll see them for a while. They need to figure what to do. If this Chato is any sort of true warrior, they'll come back for their dead."

"We could fetch Pedro and Jimmy and lay an ambush for when they return, Mr. Dunn," suggested Jake.

I shook my head. "I'll grant you that they were breaking the law by trying to rustle our beeves, Jake. However, we'll respect their dead. Besides, we've done enough shooting for a day."

Jake nodded reluctantly.

"Let's repair that fence and head home," I said with finality.

We returned home just as the sun was painting the distant clouds golden as the burning orb made its way to the western horizon. Jake and I took care of our horses, then he and I went to the bunkhouse with the intention of sharing the news with Pedro and Jimmy.

It turned out that only Jimmy was in the bunkhouse. He was chowing down on a heaping helping of steak and baked beans washed down with coffee. "Hey, grab some grub," he called out as we entered.

"Where's Pedro?" I asked.

"He had a hankering for some beer, boss. He headed to Nuecestown after we got back around mid-afternoon," offered Jimmy. "He said he'd be back sometime this evening."

I shrugged and pulled up a chair. "Jake and I ran into some Apache rustling beeves in the south pasture near the creek. We put a whipping on them, but reckon they'll come back for their dead."

"Dang, boss. How many were there?" asked Jimmy, scooping another mouthful of beans.

"Eight so far as we could count," said Jake. "We plugged four of them. The others run off."

I motioned to Jake to continue.

"We figured it was that Chato fellow that rustled beeves at the King Ranch."

"I thought the Indian wars were over," mused Jimmy.

"Guess not," I said. "Reckon I'll head into Corpus tomorrow and let Sheriff McTiernan know. Might let Archer Parr know that his constituents are being threatened. Might alert the soldiers at Fort Aransas so long as I'm near."

"You think the Apache will be back?" pressed Jimmy.

"Likely not," I advised. "This Chato fellow doesn't have a very big band. Losing four warriors should discourage him."

Jake helped himself to some grub.

"Y'all please tell Pedro about the attack when he returns. I'm heading up to the house to grab a late dinner."

With that, I stepped out into the gathering darkness and headed for the house. The irony occurred to me that the dangers faced as a lawman were hardly different from those faced as a rancher. While civilization was surrounding us, eating up the land with churches, stores, schools, and more, there was still a rough frontier that had yet to be fully tamed.

I repeated the story of the attack for Cassie, as she put together a meal for me. I watched her cook while nursing baby Carolyn. It was a beautiful sight to behold. I went over and kissed her on the back of her neck.

"You do know it's too soon, Lucas," she reminded me with a sexy wink.

"But you're looking so beautiful. I just couldn't help myself." I gave her a light hug and took a peek at my little daughter at her mother's breast. "Beautiful for sure," I said and returned to the table to sip my coffee.

Cassie winked at me. "It won't be long, lover."

I enjoyed my dinner with Sean and Bode taking turns in my lap and sampling a bite or so of what their daddy was eating. I looked forward to the day when I'd be taking them out to learn about ranching, riding horses, and hunting. It gave me a sense of what my dad must have felt, as my brothers and I grew up. Good times lay ahead.

"Do you expect any trouble from the Apache, Lucas?" Cassie asked.

"Don't think so. Still, we'll keep our guns loaded and ready." I saw that Cassie had wrapped a shawl around her shoulders. "It's going to be a chilly spring night. I think I'll close all the windows and stoke the fire."

"You can keep me warm upstairs, sweetheart," she cooed.

I reckoned that we'd at least get in some cuddling under the blankets. I stirred up the coals in the fireplace and threw a couple of logs on. The chimney would radiate some warmth upstairs in our bedroom.

Cassie tucked the boys in. They shared their very own bedroom now and were about as proud of it as a pair of toddlers could be. Cassie carried sweet Carolyn upstairs and laid her in her crib in the nursery adjoining our bedroom.

I fed the dogs before heading upstairs. They were content to sleep on a bison skin on the floor not far from the fireplace. Soon enough, all was quiet.

We were all settled in. "It's almost too quiet," I said to Cassie as I kissed her goodnight, and she snuggled under my arm.

I found myself wide awake, staring at the ceiling. I hadn't lain there very long, when I felt a chill. It wasn't the kind caused by the cold. It was the kind I got when a premonition began to grip me. Something wasn't right.

It seemed to be around midnight, when Brody and Tess took to barking up a storm. I paid them no never mind, as they were likely stirred up by Pedro returning late from his beer drinking.

The dogs persisted.

I wished that Pedro would stable his doggone horse and get settled in the bunkhouse.

Growls began to accompany the barking. Brody and Tess would never growl at Pedro. I had my ears on.

I heard a crash and tinkling of glass.

The dogs' growling and barking were replaced by whimpering, as they were hit or kicked. I grabbed my Smith & Wesson from the holster hanging from the bedpost and swung out of bed. I had no time for my trousers but pulled on my boots and strode to the bedroom door in my underwear to investigate what was going on. From downstairs, I could hear dishes being smashed, pots and pans thrown about, and furniture overturned. Another window was broken. The voices I was catching were decidedly not English or Mexican. I stepped to the head of the stairs and found myself looking down upon a fierce-looking Apache savage, a mere ten feet from me and headed my way. His painted face made him appear all the more sinister and threatening.

I raised my revolver and plugged a hole between his eyes, sending him catapulting backward. That got the attention of the rest of the attacking hostiles. Bullets soon whizzed past in my direction, but not before I'd ducked from the line of fire. I quickly replaced the bullet I'd fired. I'd need every round in my gun.

I hoped and prayed that Jake and Jimmy down in the bunkhouse had been awakened by the gunshots and would come help. Maybe Pedro would return from town in time to help. The situation sure seemed desperate.

In the midst of the gunfire and shouting, it occurred to me that Sean and Bode were in the bedroom addition downstairs. Fear for them swept through me, and I prayed that the Apache didn't find them. They'd been known to be right cruel with innocent children.

More bullets flew my direction. I ducked a splinter or two. By now, Cassie had awakened and hurried off to settle baby Carolyn, who'd been startled by the gunfire.

I heard screams; children's screams. My worst fears had been realized. Chato had found Sean and Bode.

"White man!" he hollered up the stairs. "We kill. Make even." The Apache savage's face gave off the darkest possible definition of hatred.

Two Apache hostiles held my sons; mere babes held in

the hands of savages. The boys squirmed and the warriors' grips on them tightened.

"Dadeeee!" screamed Sean.

An Apache's rough hand covered his innocent mouth.

Bode was too bewildered to be scared. At only two years old, he hadn't a full grasp of what was happening. If we all survived this, I feared he'd be scarred for life.

I took a quick look down the stairs. Two bullets sung past for my trouble. How could I save my family?

Brody had his jaws clamped on the ankle of an Apache and was soundly kicked aside for his efforts. Tess was nursing bruises off in a far corner.

Chato glared at me with fiery contempt in his eyes. A smirk, a sneer, crawled across his mouth. It was as evil a leer as might be conjured. I saw the silvery flash of the blade he drew from the beaded sheath at his waist. He waved it in front of him then swiped it within inches of my sons' faces. "White man kill Chato son, Chato kill two sons," he threatened in broken English. He paused to catch my reaction, savoring the moment of his revenge.

The Apache leader stood too close to Sean and Bode to risk a shot. What was I to do?

TO BE CONTINUED IN BOOK FIVE

EPILOGUE

THE NUECES STRIP of 1899 was still mostly a vast prairie of tall grasses and loamy-sands stretching far as the eye could see and beyond. Grasses tended to grow high enough to reach a horse's withers, though stands of live oak, mesquite, and prickly pear cactus brought to the prairie from the south, mostly by seed-carrying birds and by cattle droppings, had already begun to proliferate. Winds blowing through the wiregrass created their own special music. Brush proliferated, often creating nearly impenetrable barriers owing to the density and occasional thorniness.

The Nueces Strip, called *Wild Horse Desert* by some, reached south from the lazily flowing Nueces River all the way to the meandering Rio Grande along Texas' southern border. Its eastern extremity enjoyed the sea breezes wafting in off the Gulf of Mexico from Corpus Christi all the way to Brownsville. Nestled in hills at its northern extreme was the little town of Uvalde, while the semi-arid rolling terrain of Laredo was generally regarded as its far western reach. Rough but serviceable roads were being carved out of the Strip and mostly paralleled the railroads, which had begun to proliferate. Texas enjoyed a veritable steel spider web of interconnecting railroads. A form of creative destruction was in full flower.

Despite its mostly uninviting landscape, South Texas drew all sorts of opportunists like moths to a light bulb. Texas still remained a prime destination for second chancers, folks who'd met with rough times and looked to restart their lives. Towns, farms, and ranches sprang up at record pace. They were pressed to conquer a challenging terrain.

Much Texas history centers around the Nueces Strip. No discussion of it can ever be complete without mention that much of the most significant fighting of the Texas War for Independence was fought on and just north of the Nueces Strip back in 1835 and 1836. It was also scene to the first skirmishes of the Mexican-American War of 1846. The Strip was officially ceded to the United States by the Treaty of Guadalupe Hidalgo in 1848, though Texas had already laid claim.

The plentiful and accessible longhorns were for years the *low-hanging fruit* of the Nueces Strip economy. They were a hardy breed that could withstand the South Texas heat, fend off disease-carrying pests, and carry just enough meat on their bones to make them reasonably profitable to raise. Originally brought from the Iberian Peninsula by early Spanish priests, the longhorns eventually escaped the mostly failing missionaries, proliferated, and roamed wild and free across the prairies.

Millions of the beasts soon covered Texas and especially the excellent grazing lands of the Nueces Strip. They competed with those wild mustangs that had also been introduced by the Spaniards. Ranchers were increasingly importing and breeding meatier, shorter-horned breeds like

Brahmans, Angus, Herefords, and even Richard King's Santa Gertrudis. Of course, there had been the indigenous buffalo, millions of the beasts. They'd been a staple of the Comanche peoples' way of life until their hides were taken in wholesale slaughters to enrich eastern merchants and scions of fashion. The Texas prairies nevertheless provided plenty of feed for all.

The factor that would ultimately win the west was the family; the larger the better, as children grew up in the face of all manner of lurking dangers. Families established the ranches and farms popping up not only throughout the eastern portions of the Nueces Strip but across Texas as a whole. People sought fresh opportunities. The territory east of the 98th meridian sliced through the very heart of Texas, which was fast becoming an economic juggernaut, and the Strip was no exception. Its economy was based on growing cotton and raising cattle and horses.

Cotton was bundled and hauled to port for transport to markets in Louisiana and points east, while cattle were driven mostly to Texas slaughterhouses. And black gold gushing from countless oil wells would soon rise to be a major part of the Texas economy. Indians were pushed ever westward and to reservations, as tribes were overcome by a cocktail of socioeconomic forces, violent conflict, disease, and vast numbers of White settlers.

While the frontier grew ever westward, there remained ongoing worry about the threats posed by rogue off-reservation Comanche, Kiowa, and Lipan Apache, as well as the marauding bandits from south of the Rio Grande and lawbreaking opportunists from the east, like the Irish Mob. This all served to keep early Texans on this wild and often lawless frontier ever vigilant. It was easy to make the case for calling up companies of Texas Rangers to patrol the Nueces Strip, as they took it upon themselves to go where the military found it politically undesirable. On the other hand, the legislators in the state capital in Austin often were unable to pull together the financial means to fund the necessary companies of Rangers. They had to rely on the US Army, which could be chancy at best, as it was subject to the politics of whoever was in power and the perceiving of real or imagined threats.

Thus, the setting for the Tumbleweed Sagas: Junior's Story series is hardly any less challenging than mere decades before. Yet civilization marches inexorably onward, taming the remaining frontier.

A LOOK AT BOOK TWELVE:

PALE HORSE OF THE APOCALYPSE: JUSTICE DEFIES DEATH

Death rides hard along the Nueces.

After dismantling the Irish Mob, Texas Ranger Lucas Dunn, Jr. hangs up his badge—keeping a promise to Cassie and trying to carve out a quieter life on the ranch. But peace is short-lived. When the Apache warrior Chato storms the Dunn homestead seeking vengeance, Junior is forced back into the violence he hoped to leave behind.

Then the killings begin. A fanatical cult spreads terror across South Texas, led by a madman who believes himself the harbinger of the apocalypse. Ranches burn. Blood stains the dust. With the law unable to stop the slaughter, Junior is hired privately to hunt the killer—no badge, no backup, and no mercy. Wherever he rides, death is close enough to grab the reins.

As Spindletop erupts and oil fever grips Texas, Junior gambles again—this time on a risky well at Heaven's Gate Ranch. Fortune and violence have always ridden side by side. Justice doesn't retire

AVAILABLE MARCH 2026

ACKNOWLEDGMENTS

Authoring books simply doesn't happen in a vacuum. The author provides the creative talent and crafts the stories, but there's so much more that demands acknowledgment. There are lots of folks and places that contribute to my authoring endeavors. So, it is with *The Black Gold Mob: Capping a Crime Gusher.* It takes place in 1899 and 1900. The newly wrought exploits of the son of legendary Texas Ranger Captain Luke Dunn were at the core of the Sagas, but the Junior's Story series stands apart.

Lucas Dunn, Junior symbolizes the lawman image, the pursuer of law and order in the person of a hero, protector, knight-errant sort of character. But there's much more to him. He carries on a family legacy of grit, tenacity, rugged individualism, and bravery, nuanced with a masculine vulnerability and a search for redeeming values. He epitomizes the freedom of America's western frontier and represents a final bastion of honor in America. Hopefully, readers will find *The Black Gold Mob: Capping a Crime Gusher* an adventure worthy of their time and emotional involvement.

I've been blessed with many friends and family who have supported my writings. My wife Carolyn's reviews and encouragement were a huge help, along with very important tech support from our sons Mike and Matt. Other supporters have included Cara Miller, Jim May, Ernie Angell, Chris Haug, and my dear cousins Johnny Dunn, Jim & Cindy Holmgreen, Francette Meaney, and Eddie and

Nancy Thornton. Many more friends have contributed support at some level to the creation and publication of my books, including this, *The Black Gold Mob: Capping a Crime Gusher,* be it encouragement or advice.

Naturally, I am major grateful to the great folks at Wolfpack Publishing. The team they bring to publishing is first-rate, from editing to typesetting to cover design and the myriad tasks that lead to successful book sales.

It's only right to acknowledge my ancestors who were actual settlers of the south Texas frontier. In addition to inspiring me, they provided a quite helpful true-to-life framework as to the life and times on the Texas Nueces Strip. It was appropriate to weave them into the tapestry of my western novels. Matthew Dunn (1809-1863) immigrated to Corpus Christi from County Kildare in 1845, established a homestead on Upriver Road in Nuecestown, and served as a sutler to General Zachary Taylor's Army in the Mexican-American War. Peter Dunn (1807-1890) immigrated from Ireland in 1850 and established a blacksmith shop in Corpus Christi; John Dunn (1803-1889) ranched and grew thousands of acres of cotton; Lawrence Dunn (1837-1864) fought and died with Captain Ware's Confederate cavalry; and my great great grandfather Nicholas Dunn (1835-1912) was a rancher, drover, livestock speculator, marksman, and Comanche fighter of some repute. My cousin John Beamond *Red John* Dunn (1851-1940) served as a Texas Ranger in the 1870s under Captain Bland Chamberlain (Company H), subsequently joined a "vigilance committee," became a farmer and merchant, and curated a museum of military weapons displayed to this day in the Corpus Christi Museum of Science & History. Red John Dunn's brother Matthew Dunn also served as a Texas Ranger, and another cousin Rut Evans served as a Texas Ranger in the 1890s (Company E, Frontier Battalion, Alice,

TX). My cousin Patrick Dunn was quite successful at raising longhorns on North Padre Island east of Corpus Christi from 1883 to 1937. John Hillard Dunn (1883-1958), whose personal narrative about his family and his own adventures drove my pursuit of my Texas family, inspired my own writings, and led me to write his yet-to-be-published biography, *Tough Hombre – Recollections of a True Texan.* Finally, my grandfather, Horace Charles Greathouse, served as a Texas Ranger in 1920 (Company C, Austin, TX). Such real-life characters, coupled with actual events, have served to reinforce the historical settings for my writings.

Most of my authoring has occurred in my office as decorated to channel my inner Texan, but my creative juices have often been inspired and imagination stoked in cafés and coffee houses across America. My favorites were Hester's Café & Coffee Bar in Corpus Christi, TX; Nueces Café in Robstown, TX; Java Ranch Espresso Bar & Café in Fredericksburg, TX; PAX Coffee & Goods in Kerrville, TX; Ragged Edge Coffee House and Bantam Coffee Roasters in Gettysburg, PA; 1889 Coffee House in Helena, MT; Wild Joe's Coffee Shop, Bozeman, MT; Tumbleweed Café, Gardiner, MT; Dunn Brothers Coffee in Rapid City, SD; Postmasters Coffee & Bakery and Brio Coffeehouse in Waynesboro, PA; Birdie's Café and American Ice Co Café in Westminster, MD; Deja Brew Coffee House, New Oxford and Deja Brew at Miney Branch, Carroll Valley, PA; Baltimore Coffee & Tea Co., Frederick Coffee Company & Café, and Dublin Roasters in Frederick, MD; Qualle Café and Grounded Coffee & Bakery, Cherokee, NC; Palace Café, Amarillo, TX; and Unto Others Café, Lamar, CO. I must admit to also frequenting a few Dunkin Donuts and Starbucks around our fine nation. The décors and easy listening music in these fine establishments, combined with savory cups of coffee, tended to set me in the right creative frame of mind. They also afforded engagement with many fine citizens of our nation.

Last but not least, I'm especially thankful for the many folks who have read and enjoyed my books.

I do believe it is important to acknowledge how the old west represents the brave pioneering spirit of settlers who met the challenges and transcended mere survival to enable America to achieve exceptional growth. The settling of the American west is replete with tales of leveraging freedom for individual achievement. I hope you will agree that reliving our past—even through history-based fiction—often has the effect of pointing the way to an ever-brighter future. Might we be up to it? I hope that the inspiration I have drawn from my having walked the very earth my characters have trodden, coupled with my extensive historical research, will enable readers to fully experience the grit, adventure, and passion of my characters while sensing aromas of gunsmoke, trail dust, leather, sweat, and bluebonnets.

Thanks kindly to all of you, and do enjoy *The Black Gold Mob: Capping a Crime Gusher.*

THANK YOU

Thank you for taking the time to read *The Black Mob: Capping a Crime Gusher*. If you enjoyed it, please consider telling your friends or posting a short review. Word of mouth is an author's best friend and much appreciated.

Thank you.
Mark Greathouse

ABOUT THE AUTHOR

Multiple-award-winning author Mark Greathouse is a fifth-generation Texan devoted to history and writing western genre fiction. He has published fourteen western novels, an anthology, and a biography, as well as published western history articles in various magazines and newspapers. He received a 2025 Western Writers of America Spur Finalist Award for Short Fiction with "Prairie Dog" published in a local anthology. *Guns on the Guadalupe: Justice on the River,* published by Wolfpack Publishing, continues Greathouse's passion for weaving fiction in a historical setting. He crafts an engaging adventure, featuring an ensemble of captivating characters woven into compellingly complex subplots. Importantly, he has stayed true to the western story being America's morality story, as good triumphs over evil. Whether expressed in his epic western genre novels or adventure-laced biographies, he couples a soul-penetrating creative spirit with extensive historical research that attracts a broad spectrum of readers. Greathouse is a member of Western Writers of America and several poetry societies. He holds BA and MBA degrees. Greathouse lives in Southern Pennsylvania but travels west regularly to walk in the footsteps of his characters.

ABOUT THE AUTHOR

[illegible]

www.ingramcontent.com/pod-product-compliance
Lightning Source LLC
LaVergne TN
LVHW040218110826
845146LV00005B/1337

* 9 7 9 8 8 9 5 6 7 5 2 2 9 *